THE CONNOR PROJECT

ALSO BY LUKE WHISNANT

FICTION

Watching TV with the Red Chinese

Down in the Flood

In the Debris Field

POETRY

Street

Above Floodstage: A Narrative Poem

THE
CONNOR PROJECT

Luke Whisnant

Iris Press
Oak Ridge, Tennessee

Book Design by Robert B. Cumming, Jr.

Cover Photography by Charles Deluvio

Cover Design by Emily Forsberg

Library of Congress Cataloging-in-Publication Data

Names: Whisnant, Luke, 1957- author.
Title: The Connor project / Luke Whisnant.
Description: Oak Ridge, Tennessee : Iris Press, [2022] | Summary: "The
    Connor Project chronicles the life and loves of David Connor, a
    television journalist turned visual artist, over a twenty-year period.
    At his lowest point - his marriage defunct, his family broken, his
    career a shambles - Connor lurches zombie-like through his life, looking
    for something he can no longer name. By turns poignant and wry, funny
    and bittersweet, The Connor Project will resonate with anyone who has
    survived heartbreak and earned redemption"-- Provided by publisher.
Identifiers: LCCN 2022004068 (print) | LCCN 2022004069 (ebook) | ISBN
    9781604542615 (paperback) | ISBN 9781604548181 (ebook)
Subjects: LCGFT: Novels.
Classification: LCC PS3573.H4438 C66 2022 (print) |
    LCC PS3573.H4438
    (ebook) | DDC 813/.54--dc23
LC record available at https://lccn.loc.gov/2022004068
LC ebook record available at https://lccn.loc.gov/2022004069

Contents

As for John's sexual life during our years here in the city, suffice it to say that he dated a lot of nurses. But it doesn't suffice. Saying something like that never does suffice.

—Martin Amis, *Time's Arrow*

one

So. How do you usually get started on something like this?

I try not to preconceive it. I don't have any kind of agenda.

You just listen and go where I lead you?

Hang on a second. Let me—

Here, I'll do it. It's autofocus, you don't have to—

Just getting you in frame. Are you comfortable?

Not really.

Good.

Keep me off-balance, keep me vulnerable, is that the idea?

It's not that calculated. And this is all background. I don't plan on using any of it verbatim, not the images anyway.

So I just talk?

Something like that. I just ask questions and I listen to what you're saying and I follow up.

Okay.

So. Tell me your name.

David Loflin Connor.

Your friends call you Connor.

Yes. Pretty much everybody calls me Connor. It seems to be one of those last names that migrates to a first name. "Surname crossover" is the technical term.

Connor is Irish?

Connor is Gaelic. It means "lover of dogs." David is Hebrew, of course. "Beloved."

And Loflin?

That's a family name. My mother's maiden name. A North Carolina spelling of the Irish surname Laughlin. You meet anyone with the name Loflin, it's about 95% certain they're from North Carolina. Or their family is.

What does it mean?

It means "stranger." In Gaelic.... Is this the kind of stuff you plan to use?

Don't know yet. Go on, David Connor.

I'll be forty-three years old next February. Aquarius, before you ask. I don't believe in astrology but the traditional Aquarius personality traits are strangely accurate. Observant, unconventional, inventive. Maybe a little aloof.

What else?

My parents got divorced when I was twelve. My mom's a nurse, my dad taught philosophy. I have a younger sister. Is this the kind of thing you—

And you're an artist. A photographer and a videographer?

I don't think of myself as an artist, not in that way. I didn't go to art school or study photography. I just take photos. I got into video by working at a TV station a long time ago. Back when video meant tape, back when it was magnetic molecules on plastic film. Before bits and bytes. Whatever I know about photography and images, I picked up on my own. I'm unschooled.

Still, you do have an artistic career. You're known. People know your work.

Other artists know my work. Other local artists.

Can you describe your work for us?

Us who?

Can you describe your work?

It's just photographs and video loops. I mean, lots of different images, different kinds of images.

Are there certain kinds of ideas, themes, is there any unifying aesthetic principle, anything that shows who you are and what you're like?… How you look at the world?… Connor?

Before Breakfast

O, love. O heart, tremulous and pounding. Into the laundromat staggers David Connor, boot on the left untied, boot on the right dancing on loose left lace; peering through three swaying milk crates of dirty clothes he unexpectedly finds himself face to face with Davin Colson, a woman he'd once loved but hadn't seen in two years. Davin's dark hair, which she once wore long and straight, is dyed and dreadlocked now, and she wears no jewelry but a slim silver nose-ring. She blinks twice, recognizes him, sees he has recognized her, frowns, shuts her wide-set eyes and half-pirouettes away, tucking her chin to fold a blue bed sheet against her breast. Damn you, Connor's heart cries.

He pushes past to the very back of the laundry, but guess, O guess, what conspiracy awaits? Every blesséd washer is in use or out of order except two near the folding table, where she stands amid wheeled wire baskets brimming with damp and dry apparel. Was there ever anyone, he thinks, who loved cheap clothes more than Davin?—retro-drip-dry disco-wear and clunky wedge sandals, anything funky or tacky, anything polyester. Her closets were clogged with kitsch enough to dress a drag-queen army. Today, laundry day, she wears a pair of glittery stretch slacks and a tight red-and-black plaid shirt, and her shoes are see-thru plastic clogs. Her arms swing and jab and toss and sort through her baskets angrily, her back turned as Connor loads clothes and powder, punches WARM / LARGE and slams his quarters home–*caaah-chuff!*–lock and load, like a clip into an M-16.

"Davin," he says finally.

"David," she replies. "I thought that was you."

What bitterness, what tamped-down dormant rancor rises now, what a twisted fucked moment. We have nothing, nothing, nothing to say to each other, Connor thinks. He asks her how she is. She's fine. Living nearby? Not too far. She asks him nothing, so Connor smiles, sardonic, at the ceiling. She slides one filled basket aside and begins on a new pile. Footie pajamas. Bibs, diapers. Baby clothes.

Here are three things Connor notices in the next few seconds: (1) Davin's fingers bear no rings. (2) In her half-dozen piles of laundry there's not a single item of men's clothing. And (3) in a bassinet half-obscured by her clean clothes a drowsing blue-clad baby kicks, a tiny thing pumping his little fists; he squints and frowns and mews forlornly.

"Four weeks?" Connor guesses, as she picks him up, unbuttons the plaid shirt, and puts him to suck.

"Four months," she says. "Almost. He was nine weeks premature. I'm very lucky to have him."

Who can be heartsick holding a baby? Connor doesn't know. But Davin, blissful now, folding diapers with one hand, seems to sigh; he sees her face soften. He would like to coddle that babe himself, to ease this moment, to bow his head with hers over a tiny grasping soul. But between them in the fluorescent light looms Davin's naked breast, a place he himself knows well and used to nuzzle. Glancing away, and back, and away again, Connor hesitates. Then suddenly it's too late: looking up, she frowns and says she'd hoped with all her heart to never see him again. O so many things rush through him now that he has no way to know what to say or do. Strangely he hears himself answer that it was good to see her and he hopes she's well, and now that his clothes are going he should track down some breakfast.

"David," she calls to him, as he's leaving. He turns; "What?" he says; he looks at her: baby at her breast, a pair of pink panties wadded in her free hand, she's pointing at his feet. "Shoe's untied," she says.

At the Waffle House Connor kills an hour and three cups of bad coffee and a double order of well-done bacon. The place is deserted. He tries to scan a page or two of a day-old newspaper, but it's gibberish; he may as well be reading Sanskrit. The cook and waitress put on a little show for him, giving each other hell about their love lives. Wanda and Wayne. She wants to know why he hasn't yet married his girlfriend. He stands, back to the burners, and heaves a huge sigh. "Better safe than sorry, I reckon." Like Connor's, his eyes are the same pale blue as the gas flame. "Oh you men," Wanda says, disgusted, "you'll move your butts right in but you won't never tie the knot."

"Well, why buy the cat when the milk is free?"

"Say what?"

"You heard me."

"It's not *cat*. It's *cow*. Why buy the *cow*. Cat don't make sense, Wayne."

"Cat, cow, whatever."

"Well, it ain't fair. She deserves better. She's cooking your meals and doing your laundry."

"I usually cook *her* meals," he says, waving his spatula.

"I don't care. You ought to marry her."

"You ought to mind your own business, Wanda."

Wanda bops off to the back in a huff.

"Damned women," Wayne mutters, reaching for Connor's cup. "How bout some more coffee, bro'?"

Bro'? Connor wonders whether Wayne knows what a doppelgänger is. The two of them could almost be twins: Wayne wears a ponytail and round wire-rimmed glasses; Connor's hair is cropped short, but otherwise they look so much alike it's eerie. Connor's spooked. He doesn't want Wayne to notice. He waves the coffee off. "Stuff'll kill you," Wayne agrees.

Someday all this stuff will kill you, Connor thinks. Not eating a proper breakfast, waking up alone day after day, holding on to all this regret and sorrow, trying to figure her out. There is no figuring her out. He should head back across the street. He thinks about his wet clothes tumbling dry. He sees bluejeans, a black shirt, one red sock falling in and out of view.

Connor's Story

Connor is noting the signs. Red arrows, black capital letters, yellow flashing bulbs—they blast him head-on or catch the corner of his eye. In his father's Toyota he down-shifts and honks, creeps in heavy traffic past fast-food huts and parking lots, and reads aloud. NO ONE GETS OUT ALIVE—the marquee for a horror flick. JESUS IS WATCHING YOU, claims A-1 Used Cars. Outside a gas station: TWO 4 $1 BEST HT DOGS U EVER 8. "U2," Connor says, and keeps driving. "I'm noting the vital signs," he mumbles. Maybe he should take his pulse.

He's been at lunch with June, an indoor picnic on her living room floor. "She'd tracked me down, called me out of the blue," Connor says. "It had been years." They'd spent two hours sprawled on blue throw-pillows in front of her fireplace, drinking wine and catching up on old news. June said she'd been sorry to hear about his father, and Connor, mouth full of takeout sandwich, had nodded. He asked about her parents, her job. "Did you know I was getting married?" she murmured, as if saying it softly might ease the blow. Connor offered congratulations, said it was about time, asked if she was happy. June closed both eyes, smiled, nodded, showing her white and beautiful neck. It was her characteristic gesture, preserved perfectly from their high school days together, and Connor, seized with sudden desire, caught his breath. At the door, she kissed him, two short, one long. Then he went to get his car inspected.

"The sticker had expired. Six or seven months before, if I remember right." Connor, TV journalist, M.A.'ed in history, thirty-two years old, is singing along with his car radio: Bono and the boys doing "With or Without You," and Connor is in perfect pitch. He's let down, hacked off, a little blue. "Nothing to win," he sings, "and nothing left to lose." And he can't find a service station.

"I wasn't paying attention," Connor says now, whenever he tells his story. "I was wandering and I got turned around." All the gas pumps on this side of town seemed attached to convenience stores, 24/7, Stop Hop Shop, Kwik Pump, Grab-N-Go. No garages. "And then when I found a place with a mechanic, he was out to lunch"—a cardboard sign, at least, with real human handwriting in a big greasy scrawl. Connor climbed back in the car, cranked up the radio. "Some of the old songs, Sam," he said. They were playing all the hits.

She had looked good. Faded jeans and an oversized men's shirt with the sleeves dangling loose, and her feet were bare. "Like some bad Top 40 lyric," Connor said: "Sitting on the rug, drinking wine, me and you after all this time, doo-wah, doo-wah." June laughed, poured him another glass. They drank to the wedding. Then they drank to old flames. "Remember," Connor asked her, "remember how I used to brush your hair? For hours and hours?"

She opened her purse and pulled out a hairbrush. Connor took it, knelt behind her, lifted her heavy hair aside, kissed the back of her neck. June laughed, low, throaty, and reached back without looking and squeezed his knee. "David," she said, "when are you going to get serious?"

Connor played dumb. June told him to stop pretending. He slid the brush through her hair, tugged gently.

"Are you seeing anybody?" June said.

Connor nodded at the back of her head. "Sure."

"Are you in love?"

"I don't know."

"You don't know?"

He hit another little tangle. "Your hair's so long now. It was never this long when we were dating."

"See, I know you," June said. "I know you so well. I know just what you're like. You're in love with some girl now but it's only momentary. It's just a temporary thing."

Connor said he'd been seeing this girl five months now and June said five months was still temporary and that she knew the way he worked: he had this heroic vision, this image. To live alone and die alone and just move from relationship to relationship, a few months here, a year or two there. "Did you know bachelors over 30 are the most unhappy people in America?"

"So help me out," Connor said. "Elope with me. I'm already down on my knees here."

Then he was sorry he'd said it. He had proposed to her once before, one rainy night during their first year of college. They had planned it all out—setting up house together, quitting school, getting jobs and saving for the baby—and for a few hours they believed it. In the morning the rain had stopped and they got dressed and drove to the clinic almost without speaking. A month later they had broken up.

Now he apologized for bringing back bad memories. June tilted her head to one side and looked over her shoulder at him. "It's okay. It was a long time ago." Connor nodded. "I'm just worried about you, David. You're not a kid anymore."

"I know."

"I want you to be happy. I'm not just saying that."

"Thanks. Let's not talk about it. Tell me about your new beau."

That was the scene. She kept talking and he kept brushing. Whenever he hit a tangle, he'd set the brush down and work it out slowly with both hands. They'd finished the wine already. Finally he'd gotten up to leave, got his kiss at the door, headed back out into the heat, doo-wah, doo-wah. Driving around town in a daze.

And it seems to him later that the events of the day made some kind of sense, that they were connected. That there was some kind of meaning to what went before and what came later. "A story in two parts: The old girlfriend. The quest for inspection." He begins to tell it, not much caring who listens. Strangers, friends, his sister. Each time the story is different. He's worrying it, trying it on, shaping and arranging. Sometimes he quotes from the signs. Sometimes he leaves out the kisses. To his sister, and no one else, he mentions the abortion. He deletes and emends, digresses and backtracks, but the plot resists revision: He brushes June's hair. He meanders all afternoon. "I must have missed every garage in town—driving and thinking and not looking where I was going." He tried a half-dozen places and struck out at each. One mechanic was booked up "till tomorrow or the day after"; another yelled "Too busy" from the bay door and waved him on with a grimy hand. Two places said they'd stopped doing inspections: too much trouble. "Pump gas, check the oil, punch a cash register—that's all they know how to do anymore."

And everywhere he looks he sees the signs. ANYTHING FREE IS WORTH WHAT IT COST—a bit of wisdom from the donut shop. Outside a steakhouse, one word: ONLY—sheer mystery of the universe. And the Free Will Baptist church porta-sign claims GOD IS IN CONTROL. Which Connor believes, or at least he believes that Someone or Something is pulling the strings, connecting the dots, stacking the deck to make him the karmic butt of today's cosmic joke. "Because see," Connor says now, "this guy Ron, her fiancé—he was a sign salesman. He sold signs. You know the kind I mean." Mobile marquees for trailer parks and take-out grills, come-on's for topless bars. Do-it-yourself daily specials. "On wheels, with those black and red plastic letters you set one at a time, like Scrabble pieces, and synchronized flashing wraparound lightbulbs." The kind of thing that put your quality old-fashioned sign-painters out of business. CONGRATULATIONS JUNE & RON! And that's why Connor was noting the signs.

At last he finds a place, MECHANIC ON UTY, "duty" with the D missing. And here, Connor says, is the point of his story: it's a family garage. "There's a mom, and she's slinging a baby under one arm and slapping down the paperwork with her free hand, filling out the receipt and taking my money. And Dad's out there checking my high beams and measuring the tread on my tires. And there's a little boy, too, scraping the old sticker off the windshield and smacking the new one on. And they're all singing, singing along with the radio." Or not along, really, but singing to each other, *with* each other, a kind of call-and-response work song. And Connor is struck by this, more than struck, moved, nearly to tears. "Goddamned mawkish fool," Connor says now, laughing, but then he stood looking at this family, gritty and efficient and happy in their chosen work, and realized in a breath that he would never marry, would never have children, and that June was right: he would probably die alone in a nursing home somewhere. That's his epiphany, his moment of recognition. And lump-throated, tragic, he climbs into his car and drives away. He drifts around town the rest of the afternoon, driving abstractedly, radio low. "That's it," Connor says. "That's a wrap. Exit left, into the afternoon traffic, and fade to black."

End of story. Sort of. A half-hour later, coasting absently down a strip of burger joints and shabby storefronts, Connor sees another sign: hand-painted Greek letters,

SIGMA CHI CAR WASH $2. He pulls in on impulse. Gets out, pays. A half-dozen sorority girls in cut-off shorts and damp tee-shirts lather his car, rinse it, bend down and minister to it, brown bare arms, hair pony-tailed; and he watches, grateful, wishing June could see; he watches them sway to wipe the headlights, sees them lean laughing across the windshield like long-boned ballet dancers: plié, arabesque, pas de deux. "I watched all of it," Connor says now, "every little motion. Every dip and bounce and smile. I wanted to squeeze every ounce of significance out of that moment." It was a sign, he says, a gift, an affirmation. "See? An alternate ending to my story." Connor says he tells this to women he's just met, at parties.

How did you find her?

You really can find anything and anybody on the inter-net. Didn't you know that? But in this case I found her in the phone book. Simple.

So you talked to her? How is she?

Fine. Two kids now, both girls. Melinda and Brittany.

Good. I always hoped she'd have kids.

Because of—

Yes.

What was that like? For you, I mean.

For me it was like sitting for two hours in a hard plastic chair in a freezing waiting room. Daytime soaps. Newsweek, Redbook. Wondering how much longer. I always look back on that morning as one of my greatest failings. I had promised her that I'd go with her, hold her hand and be there for her, and when they called her name and I got up to go back with her, the nurse stopped me and wouldn't let me come in. It was against policy, she said.

If you had it to do over again, you'd insist. You'd get back there, share the experience, etcetera.

Yes. I would. I should have been there. It was part of my responsibility.

You regret it?

Not being there for her? Yes.

No, I mean the whole thing. The experience.

I'm not sure how to answer that. There's not a week goes by that I don't think about it. Things would have been completely different for me.

Maybe. I don't think you can tell about something like that.

I do. And I always felt awful about it for her sake.

She seems pretty happy now.

Good…. I ought to call her.

No, you ought not to call her. In fact, she told me this: "Tell him hi for me, give him my love, but tell him not to call me or my husband will kick his ass."

Ha.

And then she said she was serious. Her second husband, by the way. She said this one isn't as naive as her first husband was about guys like you…. What, no comment?

What can I say? Mea culpa.

It was an uncontested divorce?

Yes.

Homewrecker. Wasn't that it? She told me about it.

Yes. Homewrecker. Among other things.

On porta-signs all over town: DAVID CONNOR HOME-WRECKER.

Background

Saturday night, and the Stones are tearing down the stadium across town. Into the jammed nightclub come Connor, carrying sound, and his cameraman, Skeeter, humping the NewsCenter 9 minicam and the shoulder pack. Connor one-eighties the clientele and notes a good mix of heads, a late-twenties to mid-thirties crowd: some nose-rings, some surfer dudes, lots of big-haired babes and punks in combat boots and buttoned-down corporate types, and a pack or two of Joe-Blow beer-commercial boy-next-doors. "Fertile ground here," he decides. Skeeter hoists the camera to his shoulder. "Cool," he says. "Let's deploy," he says, "let's rock and roll." They sidle into the crowd swirling four and five deep around the bar.

Q: What was the best concert you ever saw?
A: Soundgarden.
Q: What was the best concert you ever saw?
A: Springsteen. He kicked ass.
Q: What was the best concer—
A: Elvis.
Q: Elvis? You saw Elvis?
A: Naw. Not really. I was shittin' you. I just always wanted to see Elvis.

Skeet cuts the spotlight and turns toward the bar.
"Thanks for your time," Connor says.
Soundtrack: *Let It Bleed.* The overhead speakers kick and slam with the bass drum and Connor starts picking up distortion; he adjusts his levels. It occurs to him that

Deever's crew would be backstage by now, shooting Mick Jagger from the wings, rubbing shoulders with roadies and groupies and maybe even interviewing Charlie or Keith or the singer in the opening band. He ought to be envious, but for some reason, he doesn't care. Summer doldrums, maybe—for weeks he's been on autopilot, just going through the motions.

Q: What was the best concert you ever saw?
A: Lollapalooza, man. By far.
Q: Why is that?
A: It was just, like, you know…. Aww. You had to be there. I donno.
Q: What was the best concert you ever saw?
A: Okay well it would have been one of the Dead shows but I saw 'em like thirty-five or forty times so it's hard to say which one, you know?

Turning away, Connor murmurs, "Hey, Skeet, know what a Deadhead says when he runs out of dope? … 'Man, this music *sucks*.'"

"Yeah, I heard that one," Skeet says, grinning. "Freakin' Deadheads. Hey, how about the ancient mariner over in the corner?" He nods at an old man—down-turned mouth, wispy long white hair under a sailing cap—peering into a beer. "Do him," Skeet says. "For contrast."

"We'll get to him," Connor says.

Q: What was the best concert you ever saw?
A: Led Zeppelin, Detroit Coliseum, 1973.
Q: You don't look like a Zeppelin kinda guy.
A: Neither do you.
Q: I'm just curious. I think I saw that same tour. Do you remember what they opened with?
A: Yeah, "Black Dog." They were awesome. Enormous sound. Page was wearing his infamous dragon suit. Black silk bell-bottoms with a fire-breathing dragon embroidered up one

leg, black silk jacket with a dragon across the shoulders. Wopping that sunburst Les Paul with a violin bow. What's this for?

Q: The news. How come you're not at the Stones concert tonight?

A: Oh, man, I'm all concerted-out.

"What's this for?" people always ask. "The news," Connor says, or sometimes he just points toward the minicam and Skeet half-turns so they can see the big red 9 and the LiveEye logo. People are confused, expecting the faces— reporters, anchors, the semi-famous. Connor is a nobody. He rarely appears on camera. When asked, it pleases him to say that he makes his living in the shadows, lurking.

"Hey, newsdudes," somebody yells. "Newsdudes, hey. Film at eleven."

Q: What was the best concert you ever saw?
A: I never been to no concerts.
Q: You never been to a concert?
A: Fuck off, man.
Q: Sure thing. Nice talking to you, too…. Hey, got a sec? What was the best concert you ever saw?
A: The Godfather of Soul, babe, the Numero Uno Sex Machine, I mean—gettin doooowwwn wid Mista Jaaaames Brrooown.
Q: Uh huh. Well, thanks for your time.

"Change the question," Skeet says.

"Skeet," Connor says. "The question doesn't matter. You know that. It's all form, not content. We're just cooking up some eye candy here—pretty people and light and sound and the flickering electronic fireplace."

"What is with you lately, man?"

Five years ago, finishing up his Master's thesis in History, Connor would never have imagined himself in media—least of all television. He'd gotten in through a side door, though, during a local-market one-hour special on the fiftieth anniversary of the downtown race riots; Connor had started out as historical consultant and ended up co-producing. One thing had led to another; the field was overcrowded so he'd moved around a lot; and some days found him editing, some taking sound, some producing. He hardly ever did a standup.

Q: What was the best concert you ever saw?
A: The Stones.
Q: The Rolling Stones?
A: The Rolling Stones, man. Greatest rock and roll band in the world.
Q: Why aren't you at the concert tonight?
A: Wasn't it sold out?
Q: No.
A: No?
Q: No. It's the first Stones show here not to sell out in 20 years.
A: Huh. Oh, well. Hey, you guys are Channel 9? I'm digging y'all's new Chinese anchor-girl.
Q: She's Japanese.
A: Whatever. She's a babe-and-a-half.
Q: I'll tell her you said so.
A: Cool, man. Do. Darryl. Tell her Darryl said.

"Tell her Skeet said, too," Skeet mutters, and Connor gives him a grin. "No comment," he says. He cups a hand over one ear, shoves the mic forward, yells.

Q: What's the best concert you ever saw?
A: You're breathing my air.
Q: Pardon?
A: Later, man. Speak to the hand.

She holds up her hand in a "halt" motion. Connor, despite himself, laughs. Hadn't heard that one for years.

Q: What was the best concert you ever saw?
A: I would have to say... John Pierre Rampal.
Q: Why?
A: What, aside from the fact that the man is a genius?
Q: Yes.
A: I'll tell you. See, it was Carnegie Hall, and the show sold out. They had sold too many tickets and there were about two dozen of us who didn't have seats. So they lined up some folding chairs for us on the stage, behind Rampal, and we watched the show sitting on the stage staring at Rampal's back, and everybody in the audience looking up at us.
Q: Is that right?
A: Absolutely. John Pierre Rampal Live at Carnegie Hall, on Columbia Masterworks—check out the cover photo next time you're in a record store. I'm right behind Rampal, third guy from the left. There's a woman in a purple dress on my left—my wife. She was just my girlfriend then.
A: Interesting. Okay, then—thanks for your time.

"Let's talk to some of these women, Skeet," Connor says. "And this is a big-ass boatload of white people. Just for balance, let's see if we can find a minority or two hanging around. But first, the women."

"I like blondes," Skeet tells him.

"That's a fun-fact I've never heard before," Connor says. "That's news to me."

"Kiss my ass," Skeet says, laughing.

Q: Hi, ladies. Be on TV, be famous for fifteen minutes. What was the best concert you ever saw?
A: Uh...let me think a sec.
Q: No thinking. Thinking's not allowed. It's TV. It's ephemeral. It disappears into thin air.
A: It does?
A: What a ditz. Don't interview her. Do me.
A: Shut up. He asked me first.
A: Jeeze. You'll just embarrass yourself, Angie.

Q: Thanks for your time.
A: Hey, wait a minute!
Q: Hello....What was the best concert you ever saw?
A: The one you're taking me to tomorrow night.
Q: Excuse me?

She stands there a moment, a vacuous look on her face, and then bursts into giggles. Connor, flummoxed, turns away awkwardly.

"Losing your edge," Skeet kids him.

"I'm out of practice," Connor agrees. "I admit it."

"When were you ever in practice?"

Connor essays an exaggerated and mock-mournful shrug.

A woman down the bar catches his eye. She's wearing a brown crop-top, black tights, and black ankle-boots, sitting with her legs crossed above the knee, her front foot kicking slightly in time with the music. Her dark hair is down, framing her face, and she watches him with smoky gray-green eyes as he slides toward her, Skeet following.

Q: Hi.
A: Hi.
Q: David Connor, NewsCenter 9.
A: Is that your real name? Connor?
Q: Yeah, why?
A: I thought all you TV people had fake names.
Q: Just the faces, not us grunts. I didn't catch your name.
A: It's Melissa. Think we could we do without the camera?
Q: We could, but then you'd miss your fifteen minutes of fame. What was the best concert you ever saw?
A: I'd rather not say.
Q: Why not?
A: It's not for public consumption. It's off the record. What do you guys call it? Background? Yeah, it's deep background.

Connor turns and looks at Skeet, eyebrows raised. Skeet cuts the spot, shaking his head. "Excuse us a minute," Connor says to Melissa.

He steers Skeet a few steps away, one hand on his shoulder, and bends toward his ear. "Let's call it a wrap, Skeeter," he says. "We've got plenty."

"Plenty of nothing," Skeet says, but he begins to unstrap the minicam.

"It's fluff," Connor says. "All they need is fifteen, twenty seconds." He glances at the MillerTime clock: 10:02. "You've got an hour 'til broadcast. They'll use it as the kicker, so say an hour-twenty 'til they roll it. Plenty of time for Jeanne to cob something together."

Skeet looks at him, squinting in the dim light. "You bailing, boss?"

Connor only winks.

When he saunters back in from helping Skeeter load the van, he finds Melissa has saved him a seat at the bar. She smiles at him, a little uneasily, he thinks; there's a dour air about her, a guardedness, something he can't quite articulate. Recently out of a year-long relationship, Connor decides not to be too hopeful. Go with the flow, he reminds himself, and he orders a beer from the swamped bartender. Melissa says she's never seen it so crowded here. Connor tells her he doesn't get out much. He squints at the roils of slow-motion smoke against the faux-tile ceiling and hums along with the cranked sound system: *It's just that evil life that's got you in its sway.*

"One of my favorite Stones songs," he explains.

"I can't get past the phrase 'evil life'," Melissa tells him. "To me that's an oxymoron."

Connor tries to figure this out. Maybe she means palindrome, he thinks, but that doesn't quite add up either. Up close, her eyes are uncommonly green—he suspects tinted contacts—and her gaze is steady, almost uncomfortably so. He avoids staring back; he glances at her gold earrings, her subtle brown-tinged lipstick, her short unpainted nails. She's drinking mineral water with a lime wedge. When she sets the glass back in the precise center of her napkin, he notices a dark smudge—a tattoo, a black pictograph—on the inside of her wrist.

"Is that kanji?" he asks.

She holds it up for him to examine. "Kanji is Japanese, right?"

Connor nods.

"This is Chinese."

"What does it mean?"

"I don't want to tell you."

"Why not?"

"I just don't."

"We're on background here, remember? No camera, no mic."

She sips from her water and Connor watches the lime wedge bump her brown lip. "Truth," she tells him. "It says Truth."

"Ah," Connor says.

"There was a time, not all that long ago, when I saw myself as a seeker of truth," she explains.

"Didn't we all," Connor says. He's surprised at how wistful he sounds.

"No. We all didn't. And those of us who did were just naive." She rubs her thumb slowly over the black tattoo, as if to smear it. "Anyway, I'm saving up now to have it removed."

"Don't do anything rash," Connor says, smiling. "These things go in cycles. You never know when truth will be back in vogue. Isn't that right, Howie?" he asks the bartender.

Howie smiles politely, setting a napkin, a mug, and a fresh bottle of Amstel on the bar in front of Connor.

"See, this is why I didn't want to tell you. You think

Truth is just some fad, like backgammon or Mayan astrology. But it's not."

"No, it's not," Connor agrees. "But what you're talking about, Truth with a capital T, that's the kind of truth most people are agnostics about."

"If they are, it's your fault. You and people like you."

Connor gives her a wry smile. Here it comes, he thinks.

"You go out into the world, you ask some questions, you get some answers, it doesn't matter if they're true or not, you throw them up on a TV screen and pretty soon nobody knows lies from truth, or gives a damn either."

"That's different," Connor says. "That's TV truth."

It was incredible, he thought, how many times he had heard some variation of her accusation. He had evolved several defenses, one of which was a kind of ironic agreement, trotting hand-in-hand down the same path, nodding and smiling and admitting culpability in a voice so insincere that his antagonist was often stopped short. Other times he would just dismiss the argument out of hand—"You simply don't know what you're talking about," he'd say calmly, because usually, they didn't; they were outside peering in, they saw everything in black and white. Every so often, though, he'd meet someone who he thought deserved to hear his side of it, and now Melissa strikes him as one of these. "TV truth," he explains, "is relative. It's context-based." It's all point of view and tone of voice and angle and setup, he tells her; it's all in the editing; it's sleight-of-hand, fix-it-in-the-mix; TV is the lie that helps you see the truth. "There are ten thousand masks on the face of truth," Connor says, "and we bring them to you, every single face, two dozen at a time." It was art. That was the bottom line. Everything is true, everything. He tells her he cannot think of one false thing that isn't also true.

"You really believe that?" Melissa asks.

"You can't step in the same river twice," Connor says, miming a flowing river with his extended hand.

"What the hell does that mean?"

"It means that truth is flux. It's always changing. Every time you go back to that same place in the river, it's new water under your foot."

"Truth is not a river," she says. "We're talking about two entirely different things."

"Look, I'll give you an example," he says. "I'm interviewing this guy tonight who tells me he was onstage with Jean Pierre Rampal, that he's on the album cover. Now strictly speaking—"

"Stop," she says. "Please. I don't want to hear it."

For some reason she seems to be close to tears. Connor, surprised, realizes he has not been paying attention. He cannot think how to get back to square one. He touches her arm. She recoils, sliding off her barstool out of his reach.

"I thought you were someone else," she explains.

"Excuse me?"

"It's just that you look very much like this guy I knew," she says in a rush. "Plus he worked for a TV station or a radio station or something like that." She looks into his eyes one at a time, right then left then right again, as if trying to read his thoughts. "He had some fucked-up ideas about truth, too, let me tell you."

In the sudden silence between songs she drops a five on the bar and spins off through the crowd. Connor watches her all the way to the door, willing her to turn back and meet his gaze. She doesn't.

"I was trying to warn you," Howie says during a lull. "I was trying to shoot you the high sign over here."

"What high sign?"

Howie twirls his index finger in small circles at his forehead.

"That's not the high sign," Connor says.

"Whatever."

"You think she's crazy, Howie?"

"Well, duh," Howie says. "I heard it. Some of it, anyway. She gives you all that crap about how TV is the Great Satan, but I tell you what—right now she's racing home in her little red Miata trying to catch her five-second cameo on the eleven o'clock."

"Maybe she wants to tape it for her mama," Connor says. "That doesn't make her crazy."

Howie shakes his head. "Connor, another minute and she'd have slapped your face. And for what? I'm telling you, man, I know this chick, and she's loony tunes."

Connor watches him wipe the spotless bar with a white cloth.

"She's not crazy," he says. "She just had me mixed up with someone else."

Her mistaken recognition weighs oddly on him. Not long ago on the courthouse sidewalk a persistent and maniacal bag lady had proclaimed him to be Jesus, had sworn she had seen him heal the blind. Connor had corrected her, had told her his name, had gone so far as to show her his unscarred palms. The old lady, betrayed, bitterly told him to forget it, but the encounter had haunted him; he had a sense that he'd misunderstood, that it was all metaphor, and perhaps he was oblivious to his own Christ-nature. This deal tonight had had the same quality, he thinks, a weird, addled kind of logic. For if what he believed was right—that everything was true—then maybe he *was* who she'd mistaken him for. No, he thinks, she's not crazy.

When the news comes on, he leaves his stool and stands as close to the TV as he can and motions to Howie to turn it up. The old man in the sailor cap—Skeeter's ancient mariner—mutters something unhappy into his beer and fixes him with baleful eye. Connor ignores him. He notes that Annette has put her hair back since the six-o'clock, and John has changed his tie. Otherwise, the broadcast is oddly the same, as if nothing new has happened in the past five hours. Connor finds himself sketching pretend Chinese pictograms on a bar napkin. When Deever's report on the Stones concert comes up—live from the stadium, show still in progress—he barely glances at it.

"Looks like maybe they won't get to your stuff," Howie says, nodding at the clock.

"Don't jinx it."

At 11:24, Annette smiles at the camera and says, "And finally tonight, we asked some folks who didn't make it to the Stones show what their favorite concert was. Here are some of their answers."

Connor braces himself, leans forward.

Cut to crowd scene in bar. Camera pans.

Cut to stoner girl, dreadlocks and tank top: "Soundgarden."

Cut to guy in tie and button-down: "Led Zeppelin."

Cut to bearded man: "Elvis."

Cut to Howie, popping the top on a beer bottle, smiling.

Cut to man in sweater: "I would have to say … Jean-Pierre Rampal."

Cut to Darryl: "The Rolling Stones, man. Greatest rock and roll band in the world."

Annette, laughing, voice over: "You have to wonder why he wasn't at the show."

Cut to the speak-to-the-hand woman holding up her hand. John, voice-over: "I was just thinking that myself…. So, Annette, what was your favorite concert?"

Cut back to studio. Annette, looking dreamily at John, says, "Michael Bolton."

Connor wrinkles his face. Howie laughs. "I was digging her until right then," he explains.

"Pink Floyd," John is saying. "Absolutely transcendental."

"He was tripping," Connor says. He feels unaccountably disgusted; he wonders if he's drunk. "Turn it off, Howie."

Heading out, he passes the old sailor on his way back from the men's room. Connor grabs hold of his shoulder and asks if he has a favorite concert. The old man shakes his head, but to Connor it seems he is negating the question, not answering it. "What is Truth?" Connor asks. "Do you know? Isn't everything true?"

"I got no time for your foolishness," the old man says.

Meta-Mannequin

One cloudy April Thursday, Connor finds himself between projects—restless, a little lonesome—so he heads out to the mall to take his sister to lunch.

Yellow pine pollen coats his car; it seems to swirl in the air around him. Connor suffers a miserable sneezing fit. If it would rain, he thinks. Wash some of this stuff away. The mall is like a space station: artificial light, airlock double-doors, a hermetic climate-controlled atmosphere. Once he's inside, his mood starts to lighten.

He finds Terri in Women's Wear, wrestling with a gleaming futuristic mannequin, a blank-faced chrome-plated android; she's trying to slither a blue silk dress down over this thing's big shiny breasts. Connor slips up silently. He doesn't say hey or call her name. He just says, very softly, "There's something incredibly erotic and vaguely uncomfortable about watching your sister undress another woman," and Terri, without turning toward him or missing a beat, says, "First, I'm dressing, not undressing, and second, this is a dummy, not a woman, and third, you are a freaking pervert and if you're not out of here in ten seconds I'll page security."

Connor kisses the top of her head, smelling sandalwood and mango. "How come there's no arms?"

"They're on the floor, over there," Terri says.

Connor sees them then, two entangled chrome arms with forlorn up-facing palms. "What are they doing on the floor?"

Terri makes a scrunched-up face. "To get a tight dress on a mannequin you have to detach its arms and twist its head and put it through a bunch of contortions like a freaking circus acrobat. It's harder than it looks, David. It's pretty physical. You have to struggle. You have to get personal." She shimmies the dress down over the dummy's hips.

Connor can't help but notice that this is one of the new mannequins with nipples, hard buds puckering the tight blue silk. He points this out to Terri.

"Damn it," she says. "I forgot the bra."

Connor is laughing.

"It's so creepy," she says. "On the realistic ones, the flesh-colored dummies with faces, the titties are smooth as ping-pong balls. But on these metal-heads, it's all artifice, all stylized—except for that one little thing. Some pervert designer."

"Robot sex," Connor says, and Terry says, "Don't go there. I knew you were going to go there. Christ, David."

They stare at the offending nipples.

"Robots," Connor says.

"Guess I'd better fix it," Terri says.

"Leave it," Connor says. "Let's go to lunch."

They stand in line at the mall cafeteria—Salisbury steak and salad and mashed potatoes for Connor, seven-bean salad and macaroni and cheese for Terri. They off-load their trays to a damp table. Terri looks tired, Connor thinks, and says so. "Eh," she says. "I'm just hung over. Plus it was a late gig. I didn't get home until after three."

"How's that working out?"

"Oh, you know. Same shit, different day. Playing in bars for drunks. I make about enough to keep new strings on the guitar and pay for a cab when I'm wasted."

"Don't quit your day job."

"Right. What are you up to?"

"I'm still working on that documentary about flood

stories for the arts council. Filming people who lost their homes or their farms, stuff like that."

"How's it going?"

"Almost done. Some amazing stories. Watching you dress that dummy reminded me of one."

"Yeah?"

"Yeah. Check this out. There was this kid with a canoe who was going around saving old ladies, ferrying people's possessions and rescuing cats and whatnot, and he's on the river at dusk on the second day when he sees a totally naked dead female body come floating around the bend, and he paddles over to it, full of trepidation, I imagine, being a mere sixteen-year-old boy, and he pulls the canoe alongside, and guess what it is instead of a dead body?"

"Bull," Terri says, mouth full of mac.

"I'm just telling you what he told me," Connor says.

"First of all, how did it get in the river," Terri asks, not even bothering to play along, "and second of all, those things are too damn heavy to float."

"Who knows how it got in the river?" Connor says. "There was every manner of thing in there. If you made a list of things that exist in the world, you'd have found two thirds of 'em in the river." Anyway, he continues, the boy wrestles the sodden mannequin into his canoe and off they float, meandering all night through the flood plain. Dawn finds them adrift in the estuary, where they're spotted by a National Guard Sikorsky. Against his will, the kid is winched out of the water—the rescuer rescued—and from the helicopter doorway he watches the naked mannequin shrink smaller and smaller as she heads out to sea in his old blue canoe. The End. "What do you think of that," Connor asks his sister.

"I think some people will believe anything whether it happened or not," she says. "Now if you dressed mannequins for a living, David, you'd soon get over these patriarchal notions about water nymphs and succubi and women as ornamentation, and find yourself a real girl with some brains in her head and settle down and get married."

"I don't want to get married," Connor says, "and you don't either. Nobody in their right mind would want to get married."

"I might," Terri says. "Maybe."

"I don't see you out scouring the wilds for a fiancé."

"How are you spelling that?" Terri asks. "Maybe I'm looking for a fiancée"—she traces the double *e* in the air with her finger—"not a fiancé."

Connor just shakes his head.

"Have a little faith."

"Faith in what?" Connor asks her. "Let's face it—we're both fucked. Cynics, pessimists. Freak-ass products of a broken home."

Terri says she hates the phrase "broken home."

"Broken, dysfunctional, fucked. Take your pick. Deal with it, sis."

"Whatever, David," she says.

Connor lifts one corner of his mouth, more ironic grimace than smile.

"Now let tell you a *real* mannequin story," Terri says, poking at her mac and cheese. "This is like that woman on Oprah who had all those plastic surgeries and implants and hair extensions trying to look exactly like Barbie. Remember Kathi, from Cosmetics? that I tried to fix you up with?"

"I do," Connor says, slicing his steak.

"Well, she's *turning into* a mannequin—I'm not kidding." There's a brand new mannequin, a real pretty one, in Petites, Terri says, and Kathi stands around admiring it for whole minutes at a time; she buys whatever outfit it's wearing that week; and when she thinks nobody is looking she cocks one hip and bends her elbow just so, mirroring the mannequin's pose. She even got the same haircut and dye job. "Which is idiotic," Terri says, "and do you know why?"

"Yes," Connor says, proud of himself for figuring it out, "because it's a wig, and tomorrow morning you might put a totally different color and style wig on that mannequin and then Kathi'd be out fifty bucks for her now-superseded hairdo."

"Smart boy. But more like a hundred."

Connor's only date with Kathi had been five weeks ago. She'd worn black jeans and a black button-up blouse; it was the only time he'd ever seen her out of her white Clinique smock, and oddly, he found he preferred the smock. She seemed distant and sad and a little desperate to him; they didn't really click, but that didn't prevent them from rolling around on her chintz sofa for a few hours, half-undressed under a moonlit window. Connor remembers her bare shoulders, her collarbones, her lips, her small soft breasts. But now, when he considers this flesh-and-blood woman obsessing over a plastic dummy—and okay, he thinks, this is weird, I admit—he has no desire to see Kathi, the meta-mannequin, but he's dying to see the template, the Platonic form, the mannequin itself. "Let's go by and sneak a peek at it," Connor says, but Terri looks at him like he's lost his mind. "What's wrong with you?" she says. "It's just a damn mannequin."

"Well," Connor says.

His sister is staring at him. Deflated, he takes up his spoon and gazes at his concave reflection in the dull metal. His face is distorted, monster-like.

"Freak-ass," Terri says.

Connor goes back to the mall in the early evening, half an hour after Terri has clocked out. It's raining. Whirlpools of yellow pollen swirl down the parking lot storm drains. Slung under his windbreaker are a Nikon loaded with 400 ASA black & white and a Pentax with color slide film. He tilts his wet face up to the rain and breathes deeply.

Inside, he approaches obliquely: through Lingerie, re-treating through Sportswear, meandering down the aisle across from Cosmetics, with its mirrors and glass counters, its white-smocked makeup technicians. Kathi is not working, he notices, and then he sees the Petites mannequin: a small, graceful thing standing with hips slightly cocked, a distant look and a bit of a Mona Lisa smile. It's wearing a pair of white capri pants and a familiar black button-up blouse. Connor raises his Nikon, focuses and clicks. He gets off half a roll before a salesclerk asks him what he's doing.

"I'm a friend of Kathi's," Connor says, backing up and shooting.

"Kathi has the day off. Is there something I can help you with?"

Connor keeps shooting. He sees shots of mannequin faces enlarged two or three times life-size, blown up so big and grainy that you can't tell them from real women. He sees piles of arms and legs and torsos. He sees himself in a canoe with his arms around a muddy mannequin, drifting out to sea. He imagines his photos framed in black, with wide white mats, hanging on a gallery wall.

"Sir. Is there something I can help you with?"

Connor keeps shooting his mannequin.

I saw that show. Your mannequin photographs.

What did you think?

I thought the photography was good, in an interesting way. Unrefined. Unpretentious.

Thanks.... But?

But the subject was a little hackneyed for my tastes. Women as mannequins, that whole objectifying women thing. It's been done to death.

By women artists. Not men.

Maybe so. Still, the subject is kind of a cliché.

Well, what do you expect. It was my first show.

You were what? Twenty-five years old?

Twenty-six.

Early success in the local art scene. Big sales, patrons, groupies. Stop laughing.

Art groupies. Girls with black fingernail polish and lots of mascara.

Speaking of mascara....

Yes?

You never went out with the Clinique girl again? Kathi?

Hmm. Maybe?

You don't remember?

This was all a long time ago. Ten years. Maybe fifteen.

Still, how could you forget a second date with a woman who aspired to be a mannequin?

Well ... I try to block out the crazy ones, you know? Otherwise I get to feeling like a damn lunatic magnet.

Maybe you've got good reason to feel that way. What was the girl at the bar's name? Melissa?

Yeah. Melissa.

Well, there you go.

What are you saying? She wasn't crazy, just a little off-balance. It's like I told Howie—she just had me mixed up with someone else, someone who'd screwed her over somehow, and it upset her. That doesn't make her a lunatic.

What about the bag lady, the one who thought you were Jesus?

Well, yeah, maybe she was a lunatic. But street people, you know, they latch on to anybody. I just happened to be handy that day. That doesn't mean I'm a lunatic magnet.

Hope not.

Hey—

On the Street

Connor was heading home from a disappointing blind date—a drop-at-the-door, I'll-call-you-sometime good-night—when he saw something he'd never seen before: a motorcycle lying in the road.

"Just stating it like that, it doesn't sound like anything," he says now. "But you have to see it the way I saw it."

A thunderstorm had knocked out power earlier, so the black street was still wet and all the streetlights were out; the whole city seemed dark and unfamiliar to him. His was the only car for miles; at least that's what it felt like. He had taken a shortcut, turning off the boulevard onto an empty backroad, and a quarter-mile later, around a sharp curve, there it was: a motorcycle lying on its side, headlight on and amber hazard lights flashing. He nearly had to stand on the brakes to keep from running it over.

"The odd thing, to me, was how beautiful it was, this image. It was a big bike. Fast. But it was down. It was like something running fast had been shot down and was lying there gasping for air or something. Like it was breathing. The engine was off but those yellow lights kept blinking. The black street. The yellow lights. The white halogen headlight peering off into the distance."

He got out of his car and started yelling. Hey. Anybody hurt? Are you okay? Where are you? —Nothing.

"It was right on top of the double yellow line. It looked to me like maybe he took the turn too fast and the bike slid out from under him and he got thrown in the ditch or something. He must have been hurt—maybe unconscious or even dead. Otherwise why would he have left the bike there, with the lights going?"

Connor leaned back in his car, grabbed his phone and dialed 911. While he talked he began walking around the bike, spiraling outward. It didn't make sense to search behind the bike, he thought—the momentum would have thrown the rider forward or slightly to one side—but he couldn't be sure which way the rider had been going, so he kept circling.

"A Yamaha 850," he said into the phone.

"ZOOM-1," he said. "A vanity plate."

"ZOOM," he said. "Just like you'd think. Z as in Zoo. Double O as in Oscar. M as in M&Ms, hell, I don't know. A hyphen followed by the numeral one."

"I can't see what color it is," he said. "It's dark out here. The power's still off. Maybe it's red? It looks red."

"I won't," he said. "Okay. Okay."

He thought about moving his car off the road but instead went back and punched his blinkers. They flashed the same shade of amber as the motorcycle's lights.

He yelled again. No answer.

How far could someone be thrown from a speeding motorcycle? Especially if, instead of a collision with another object, the bike simply slid out from under you?

"It didn't add up. No sign of a rider. After a few minutes I decided this guy had just set it down and walked away. It was the only thing that made sense."

From two directions he could hear the sirens—mournful, angry. Ambulance, firetruck, two cop cars, that was his guess.

Where are you?

His cell phone was ringing. Connor punched "ignore," popped his trunk and pulled out his camera bag. Stills or video? The Sony was the first thing to fit his hand—

"—which actually was perfect, when I thought about it later, because video was what you wanted for this image.

The thing that made it so visceral, so compelling, was motion in the midst of stasis. I mean the machine was dead. Just lying there. But the blinkers, the lights going at this precise interval, like a visual metronome…. I'm trying to say this right … it had to be video. So that's what I shot."

He shot video until the cops got there.

Connor says he is all about serendipity. Found Art is his forte, the aesthetic of the unexpected. If you ask Connor montage or mise-en-scène, it's mise-en-scène, every time. "What's in the frame," he says. "That's all you need. No setups. Just what's in the frame."

But he usually finds a theme, a controlling idea. "Wo/man-nequins." "Inside/Out"—one of his favorites. "Just Begin." "Weathered." And "On the Street"—for which he's been collecting images off and on for a few years. Graffiti. Hopscotch. Shards of torn-up tires strewn across the pavement. Garbage. Old shoes, always only one shoe—"Ever noticed that? What do you think happened to the other shoe? Why is it always only one shoe?" An oil can, green and silver, rolling in slow half-circles in the wind, crossing lanes of traffic, spinning end around end, bumping into the gutter, the rainbow of leaked oil firing in the sunlight.

And last year the weirdest thing: just outside his apartment, on the street, cops congregated around a discarded pair of jeans. Women's jeans, maybe a size two, maybe a four, it was hard to tell from his doorway. "What about this?" a cop called to him. "You know whose these are?" Connor shook his head. He was telling the truth, but for some reason he felt he was lying; he felt unaccountably guilty, though no woman had visited his apartment for weeks. He watched a cop climb onto the bumper of his patrol car with a camera to take an overhead shot of the jeans. They were light blue, he noticed; "acid-washed" was the phrase that came to mind, a style a lot of women and girls were wearing that year. The cop took a few more pictures, then his partner began laying red tape on the asphalt, outlining the jeans like a body at a murder scene. Connor thought, Are you freakin' kidding me? He went back inside for his camera.

The first lights were red, from the ambulance. They reflected off the same part of the street as the yellow flashers. Connor watched the two colors cycling into a weird rhythm—the reds spun in a wide elliptical pattern over the pavement and crossed over the upturned bike in the intervals between yellow flashes. The lights pulsed, perfectly synchronized, spinning like interlocked gears; but when he turned away to speak to the medics, then turned back, he saw the two lights had fallen out of sync. Then blue police car sirens exploded the pavement into fireworks, chaos. People were yelling over the squawk of radios. Connor shut down his camera, set it on the hood of his car. He took two steps toward the cop cars. He said, "I can't f—"

Then—

"Here he is!" somebody yelled.

Everybody turned. Connor saw a dozen flashlight beams converge in the ditch across the road.

Ten minutes later, head down, he watched the ambulance lights skitter away in the black mirror of the pavement. He watched someone kneel down and switch off the motorcycle headlight and blinkers. Then suddenly the streetlights popped back on and everyone looked up, blinking. Someone asked Connor for ID, for his current address, for his phone number. Someone asked if he were okay. He found himself trying to explain something to a police detective. He heard someone calling in a tow truck request; someone else called out, Flatbed, not a tow truck, tell them a flatbed. Connor affirmed that he was a photographer, a video artist. He swore that he had looked, he had looked for a solid five minutes. He said it was too dark, it was the blackout, it was darker than hell in that ditch. He kept seeing them bringing the body out, a kid in a tattered black teeshirt, no helmet, one white tennis shoe twisted askew.

"When you see something like that," Connor says now, and then he trails off, thinking.

"When you see something like that … okay, of course there was a compelling human factor there, the same thing anybody would have felt—horror, empathy, whatever, just trying to find the guy and get him some help…. But there's this other dimension, this parallel thing for me: the image. The power of that image, that yellow flash on the wet black pavement. A yellow light on a wet street—I read this one time—is the most beautiful image there is." Maybe that's true and maybe it isn't, he thinks. Maybe I'm just rationalizing. "Anyway, I saw this thing, this image, and I saw them bring the body up on a stretcher, and they took my name and address and they took my camera and told me it was evidence and I could get it back later, and they told me to move along now, the show was over, nothing left to see here, and all I could think about was that I had to call somebody and tell them."

So he called his sister. She sounded drugged, distant, as if she were sleeping underwater. "What is it?" she wanted to know. "Is it Dad?"

Connor said it was not. "Nothing's wrong. I just had to tell you about something."

"Because, see," Connor says, "Terri is like I am. She has an appreciation for the random, the unexpected. She likes images. She would understand about a yellow light on a wet black street." So he started in on his story.

"It's like that thing Dad always used to ask us, when we were kids, remember? About grandma and the Mona Lisa?"

"Sort of," Terri mumbled.

"Yeah, you remember. You're with grandma in the Louvre when it catches on fire. Grandma is over here, the Mona Lisa is over there. Which do you save?"

"David," Terri said. "I have to work in the morning. For God's sake."

"You save Grandma. Right? That's what we always said. And Dad would just shake his head like we were idiots. But Grandma. You couldn't let Grandma burn up, could you? But wait now. What if the choice was between some stranger—a young guy, say, somebody you didn't know—and the Mona Lisa. What if the young guy was already dead, only you didn't know it? What if—"

Connor stopped, listening. Nothing. After a moment he heard the slightest snore. He hung up.

The amber digits of his car clock read 12:21. Connor circled the block, thinking, then pulled back onto the boulevard. When he caught a redlight he flipped his phone open and looked at his log. He found a call to the woman he'd taken out, made earlier in the evening when he was trying to find her house. He hesitated. Then he highlighted the number and hit SEND.

"I woke her up too. And I didn't know her well enough to wake her up. But I started talking anyway."

He told her what he was feeling. He told her everything. His love of color and motion. His horror at seeing the dead rider. His human failing. It came out all fumbling and disjointed. "I can't explain it," he told her. "I know I'm not making any sense. I mean… I don't even know what I'm trying to tell you, really…."

"Where are you?" she said.

"I don't know," Connor said. "Out on the street. On the boulevard, you know. And it's late and I'm sorry to bother you."

He heard her sigh.

"Come back," she said. "Come back and I'll put some coffee on. It's not that late. We can talk. You're upset. You can tell me all about it."

"Really?" Connor said.

"Really," she said.

"Okay," Connor said. "Yeah. That'd be good."

"I'll go unlock the door."

Connor said bye, snapped shut his phone, flipped on his blinker for a U-turn. The light was green so he went.

Are you a ne'er-do-well, Connor?

Me?

Yes, you.

I always think of ne'er-do-wells as guys who hang out all day in bars and pool halls or street corners, hustling nickels and dimes. Disreputable guys. Guys without jobs.

But you don't have a job.

An official job, with a salary and benefits? No. Not currently. I'm doing okay, though. I own some rental property. As you know. And I sell a few photographs and sometimes I shoot corporate videos. So I'm not a ne'er-do-well.

But you've dated a lot of women.

A few.

A lot. How many?

I haven't counted. Like what's "dated"? Are you counting every single woman I ever had dinner with? Every woman I kissed? Every one I slept with? What?

Let's just say there have been a lot. So many that an impartial observer might say you are the dictionary definition of the phrase Fear Of Commitment.

I don't think that's it. I think—

Of course others might say that you just love women.

Oh hell fire. That's not—

How did a nice boy like you turn out to be such a badass?

I'm not a badass. I don't even know what you're talking about.

How did you get to be the way you are?

You tell me.

I have a theory, of course.

Of course.

My theory is that you grew up lacking a male role model.

My dad was a male role model.

Exactly. Your dad is exactly what I'm talking about. Your dad is a notorious womanizer, he's been divorced three times, he's a narcissist, he dates girls half his age—

Yeah? So?

Come on.

Okay, all that's true. No argument. But I didn't say he was a positive *role model. All those things made him a negative role-model. Seeing firsthand the way he was with women made me determined not to be like him. And besides that, he and Mom split up when I was eleven years old, so he wasn't around enough to be a big influence on me.... What? You don't believe me?*

I didn't say that.

You don't believe me. I can tell. You don't believe that he was my negative role model.

I believe that you *believe that.*

Wow. I don't know what to say.

I'm remembering all this. I'm going to use it.

Oh no you're not.

Just watch me. You'll see.

Just leave my dad out of it, okay?

two

University Billiards

"So I was new at this school," Connor said over his shoulder.

"I hear ya," Skeeter said.

"I didn't know many kids. Junior high school—ninth grade and never been kissed. A bit of a late bloomer. It was opening night for the drama club play. Even then I was a behind-the-scenes kind of guy. I was working lights, running the sound board." He watched as Skeeter chalked his cue. Blue dust drifted down on the worn green table. "The show was over and we were striking the set, cleaning up, goofing off. I was taking a break, sitting cross-legged on the stage and minding my own business when this girl comes up, a girl I'd never seen before, and she plops down right next to me and starts flirting with me and next thing I know she's lying down with her head in my lap, looking up at me, smiling, and I'm totally about to lose it."

"Was she cute?" Skeeter asks.

"Aww, man, she was cute as a little dollbaby," Connor told him, "curly hair and a little turned-up nose and dimples and she was wearing cutoff jeans and this halter-top thing with a bare midriff and I didn't know what to do at all; I mean I knew she wanted me to kiss her, that was pretty apparent, but the assistant stage manager was sweeping up downstage right—"

"Wait, what do you mean 'sweeping up'?"

"I mean literally," Connor said, "he had a push broom and was sweeping the stage and wasn't even trying to hide that he was watching us; I mean he was sweeping in circles and craning his neck and grinning this crazy grin at me, and there was somebody else offstage in the wings breaking down a set or something and it just wasn't much of a venue for a first kiss."

Skeet broke with a tremendous *crack* and balls scattered and caromed but nothing dropped; "Open table," he said, and Connor stepped up and bent down and sighted and lined up his shot, still talking: "So she was lying there looking up at me and smiling and I'm just looking down at her and continuing the conversation, something inane, teenaged babble, purple people eaters or something, man, and"—Connor knocked in the two-ball—"eventually she had to reach up and put her hand on the back of my head and literally pull my face down on top of hers until we were looking cross-eyed at each other and laughing"—Connor sunk the six in the side and turned to the four—"and then we were kissing, right there on stage, and it went on and on and on, like a five minute lip-lock without coming up for air or anything." Connor sank the four and walked around the table and saw the he couldn't reach the one or the five but could bank the three in the corner, so he did, and then came back for the one in the side. Skeet said in a girly voice, "And you thought, *So this is kissing.*"

"More like *holy crap*, Skeeter," Connor said, "especially the way she was rolling her head around in my lap," and Skeet gave a soft "Whoooohoo" and Connor just barely tapped the seven and it rolled and hung on the lip of the corner pocket and teetered and then fell, but he wasn't watching; he was already stalking around the table to line up the five. "Don't do this to me, Connor," Skeet said, "not again, man," but Connor just waved his cue toward the far pocket, a straight shot right down the rail, and popped it with backspin and rattled it home. "So then this girl gets up and flounces off, like all she wanted was one kiss and that was it, and she disappears and I don't even know her name." "Whaaaa?" Skeeter said, "man, you're shittin me, you didn't get her name?" and Connor said, "I told you, man, I was new in this school and didn't know these kids." He called his last shot, lining up the white ball and the black ball and patting the side pocket. It was a reasonably easy shot: cut the eight-ball, just barely kiss it, he thought, and he pulled back his cue. The eight spun into the pocket and Connor started to turn away to tell Skeet "rack 'em," but then he saw the cue ball rolling still, rolling straight for the corner, and—shit—there it went: scratch. Connor laid his cue across the rails, put his face in both hands, and shook his head. "Heysu Cristo," he said.

"No help for the wicked," Skeet said. "Rack 'em up, my friend."

Connor started racking. It didn't take long since all the high balls were still on the table.

"That's a pretty good story, though," Skeeter said, re-chalking his cue, "that first kiss story. Better than mine."

"That's not the whole story."

Two hours later he was at the cast party looking for this girl. Somehow she'd gotten away from him and he was starting to wonder if he'd been dreaming. Then he saw her, standing all by herself across the room; she was wearing slacks and a long-sleeved cotton blouse with every button buttoned. Connor dropped all his cool and bee-lined to her. "This is the hard part to tell," he said. "I mean it's embarrassing. I stood there talking to this girl—a girl whose name I still didn't know—and she totally gave me the cold shoulder, acted like she'd never seen me before. I couldn't figure it. I kept kind of sliding her sideways without really meaning to, kind of backing her up into a corner, and finally I said something a little pathetic and disappointed, something like 'You're not being as nice to me as you were earlier tonight,' and she said 'What are you talking about?' and, man—"

Skeeter is leaning on his cue waiting to break. He raises his eyebrows: go on.

"For the first time in my life I made a move. If she could do it, I could. I just leaned down and kissed her.

Talk about huevos!" Connor shook his head. "She pulled back and she looked at me really weird and then she smiled and leaned back in and kissed me back, but not like before; it was like a deep kiss but quick, and then she said 'I'll be right back' and she slipped out the door and I didn't see her again that night."

Skeeter turned to the table and broke. High balls dropped in three pockets. "Stripers," he said, and Connor watched him backpedal around the table, sussing out the lay. "You were new in the school," Skeet said. "That was a given."

"Correct."

Skeet leaned over the table and drew a bead on the eleven. "Twins," he guessed. "You kissed twins without knowing it."

"Yes."

The eleven bounced off the edge of the corner pocket. Connor wasn't watching. He'd just seen his father come in, holding the heavy plate glass door for one of his students, a girl named Tamara Fox. They bought a rack of balls and set up two tables over. His father nodded at Connor and Connor nodded at his father, and Tamara waved her fingers.

"You know that girl," Skeet asked out of the side of his mouth.

"I've met her. It's my shot?"

"It's your shot," Skeet agreed.

Connor told himself he was not going to get hung up on this. It was the kind of weirdness he had grown used to and it only gave him pause for a moment. He turned his back and did a half-orbit of the table. "What am I, low balls?"

"Solids. Yeah."

Connor missed a bank shot on the four-ball.

"Twins," Skeet reminded him.

"Mary and Marcie McGruder," Connor said, a little wistful. "Mary was the wild one. Dropped out pregnant in eleventh grade. Marcie was honor roll, student council, pre-med, all that stuff. I had no idea."

"This explains a lot," Skeet announced.

"You think?"

"Connor, man, this is why you're so fucked up about women," Skeet said. "Don't you see it? Your first kiss and you got 'em both—the virgin and the whore, Eve and Lilith, the yin and the yang, man—on the same day, both vibes coming out of identical packages. It confused you— gave you unreasonable expectations. How could any one woman live up to that?"

"You're pretty funny, Skeeter," Connor said.

"You know I'm just yanking your chain here." Skeet knocked in the twelve and turned toward the ten. "But I will say one thing, Connor. These girls were good luck for you, this Marcy and Mary. Ever since then you've had good luck with girls whose names start with *M*." Skeet glanced up and winked. "Marcy, Mary, Melinda—"

"—Melinda? What Melinda?"

"Miranda, I mean—-the blonde with the big—"

"Oh, yeah—Miranda."

"—Melissa, two Melissas now that I think of it— damn, Connor, you don't need any more *M*'s; you need to move on to some other letter of the damn alphabet."

Skeet stopped to watch Tamara Fox bend over the table in her tight bluejeans. Connor looked too and saw his stern father watching him. He didn't care. He was thinking, *Allison, Amanda … Ashley, Belinda, Caryl, Christine … Davin, Ellen, oh yeah, Candi …. F, who's F? F… F… F….*

A Happiness Koan

Connor's father, a bitter, jaded professor of philosophy, world-weary and cynical, with a dour down-turned mouth, has an inexplicably silly side: he tells hideous jokes, the kind based on bad puns. To him the pinnacle of hilarity is Abbot & Costello's "Who's on first?"; Groucho and Chico doing "There ain't no such thing as a Sanity Clause" is better than Shakespeare. He specializes in wordplay and non-sequiturs, preferably delivered in cheap cowboy hats, of which he has a collection. Sometimes when Connor comes over for dinner he'll tell his first joke in a little boy's red felt cowboy hat, a hat so small that it sits barely balanced on the crown of his head, and when he finishes the punchline, deadpan, with everyone groaning, he'll take this thing off and carry it to the hall closet to put it away and then he'll return in a white foam *America's Team* Dallas Cowboys hat two sizes too big, the kind of thing they might pass out on Hat Night at the stadium; he'll pull it down over his eyes and squint and he'll say something like this:

"So this homeless guy is passing through town looking for work and he sees a sign outside the cathedral that says *BELL RINGER NEEDED*. Stop me if you've heard this one. The guy thinks, Bell ringer! I can do that! So he bursts through the door of the bell tower and goes flying up the stairs—my new job, wow, this'll be great—and when he gets to the top he sees there's no pull rope on the bell, so he throws himself against it, *wham!* with his head, and sure enough the bell rings out loud as heck but the guy is knocked unconscious and thrown out of the bell tower and falls six stories down into the town square to his death. The chief of police runs up and turns the guy over and says in desperation, 'Does anybody know this stranger?' And the priest takes a long look at the man, and then he says"—and here Connor's dad waits maybe two seconds, eyebrows raised, and then: "'No, but his face sure rings a bell'."

And when the groaning is over he goes back to the closet and exchanges the white foam hat for a Kelly green Stetson stenciled with the slogan *Irish Cowboys Know How to Poke* and he walks back into the kitchen and starts right back up with "So the next week the dead bell ringer's twin brother comes through town. The exact same thing happens: he sees the sign, he runs up the stairs, he flings himself at the bell, rings it but is knocked unconscious and falls to his death—"

"No, Dad, no," Connor is saying.

"—and the chief of police turns him over and says in desperation, 'Does anybody know this stranger?' And the priest takes a long look at the man and says"—Connor covers his eyes with both hands, waiting— "'No, but he's a dead ringer for that other guy.'"

He never laughs at his own jokes. He just goes and hangs up his hat.

When Connor was thirty-three, he met a woman named Serena, who on their first date during a conversational lull set her fork down, winked, and said, *a propos* of nothing, "So one day Roy Rogers buys a brand new pair of cowboy boots—ostrich skin, six hundred bucks from Neiman Marcus—and he leaves them outside the door of the ranch house 'cause Dale doesn't want him tracking dirt in on her nice clean floor, and during the night a mountain lion comes snooping around on the porch and tears up the new boots. Stop me if you've heard this one."

Connor blinked, then told her to go on.

"Roy finds his half-eaten boots in the morning and he's so mad that he saddles up Trigger and starts tracking and he spends all day tracking that mountain lion and finally he finds it and shoots it dead and throws it across his saddle and rides back to the ranch. Dale is waiting for him at the door, and do you know what she says?" Serena cleared her throat and then crooned, to the tune of "Chattanooga Choo-Choo," "'Pardon me, Roy—is that the cat who chewed your new shoes?'"

"So of course I introduced them," Connor says now. "It seemed like the right thing to do."

A year later his dad and Serena bought a condo and moved in together. Connor wondered whether having a girlfriend twenty-six years younger had created in his father intimations of mortality; he didn't know, but in any case his dad had decided to live forever or die trying, and he'd overdone it, riding his exercise bike two or three hours a day until he developed an inflamed prostate, so he was spending a lot of time floating in the pool with his arms draped over an orange foam tube. Connor stood with him in neck-deep water while they talked about chance and opportunity and happiness—the kind of conversation he couldn't ever remember having, ever, with his father. Happiness. "So maybe Socrates was wrong," his father concluded, "about the unexamined life. Maybe life doesn't need to be examined, just lived. *Live* your life. Be happy." Connor said he thought that happiness was overrated, and that in any case he had his work and maybe that was enough. He told his dad that he was making a film, a film about fathers and sons, and he'd like to shoot him telling one of his famous bad jokes.

Connor's dad smiled and shook his head just the slightest bit. He looked over at Serena, who was listening from the shallow end in a Kelly green bikini, and she said, "We don't tell jokes anymore. We tell koans." She stood up and with one graceful finger drew a figure-eight on the surface of the water and said, "Here's a happiness koan for you, David. Stop us if you've heard this one. Two blondes, one on either side of the river. First blonde"—she cupped her hands around her mouth and did a high bimbo Valley-girl voice calling across a wide expanse—"*Yoooo-hoooo! How ... do you get ... to the other side?*"

And Connor's father, sixty-two years old, cupped his hands around his mouth and answered in falsetto as the other blonde: "*Duuuhhhhh!!! You're already ON the other side!*"

There was the briefest of pauses. "And then he did something I had never seen him do," Connor says, "ever. He started laughing, laughing at one of his own jokes. He dropped his deadpan face and shook his gut laughing." Serena, laughing too, glanced at Connor: *You're already ON the other side. Get it?* Connor smiled a little uncertainly. He decided he would have to think about it.

So your dad ended up with your girlfriend?

She wasn't my girlfriend.

No?

No. We just dated a few times.

When you say "dated"—

I mean we went to dinner and maybe a movie or something. We might have fooled around some but nothing serious.

Still, wasn't it weird to see her with your father?

It's sort of gotten to the point where nothing about him was weird to me. You know? It's like, yeah, I see how it ought to be weird, but I just stopped thinking like that.

Were you jealous?

It's like this. I never saw him happy before that. Never. Content, maybe. Certainly not miserable. But even when he would tell his jokes, it was more just a kind of ritual. He was serious, you know? A serious man. So to see someone like that finally find some joy, some real happiness—how are you going to be jealous of whatever brought him that?

It was a brain tumor?

Yeah. Edema leading to intracranial hypertension, followed by coma and eventual shutdown. Sudden onset but lingering outcome.

You miss him.

Yeah.

Castro, Mi Amor

Connor watches footage of his father. Here are Super 8 home movies, black and white: Dad at the hospital holding his new baby boy, Dad pulling up to the garage in his brand new Buick. Here are VHS tapes, color and grainy: his dad snagging a foul in church league softball; his dad at the beach in a floppy hat, scratching his unshaven chin and gazing at the horizon, somber and contemplative. Here's digital video: dad teaching class, the old professor pacing a slow circle around a lectern, gesturing and nodding, stabbing a stub of chalk at the blackboard. Connor pauses, reverses. His father is saying something about the Pre-Socratics, about how the ancient Greeks had more highly evolved ideas than most modern Americans. "What is the cosmos made of?" he muses. "Some of the first people we would call philosophers—literally, 'lovers of wisdom'—struggled with this question and came up with some pretty good answers." He then explains some of the cosmic answers: fire, water, atoms, pure numbers. Connor thinks this scene might make an opening to his project, so he jots down the counter number, then resumes play.

His mother says directly to the camera, "Gene, happy 65th birthday." After a pause, she adds, "You son of a bitch…. You can edit that part out, right?"

His father's former mistress says, "I'll always love you, Gene, even though you broke my heart twice. Happy birthday."

His father's third wife, a woman a few years younger than Connor, says, "I love you, Sugarbabe. Happy happy birthday, and many many more," and then she blows the camera a kiss.

His sister says, "Happy birthday, Daddy. How the heck did you get so old? Just kidding! I remember when you used to read me to sleep every night from the *Iliad*. What a crazy thing to read a child. All those people hacked and slashed to death.... No wonder I had nightmares. Well, anyway, happy birthday—sorry I couldn't be there."

Connor shuts off the monitor, grabs his jacket and heads for the hospital.

His mother works the neonatal ICU, a ten-hour shift, four days on, three off. To get there you walk past a big window looking in on the normal nursery, a dozen or so newborns sleeping, crying, kicking, being held to the window by student nurses, being *ooh'ed* and *ah'ed* over by friends and family standing in the hall. Connor occasionally finds himself drawn to this window, gawking at the babies, yet at the same time he feels something not entirely right about looking; he feels in some ways like a voyeur, that without any claim of kinship or acquaintance there isn't much difference between looking at babies in a hospital and looking at chimps at the zoo. It was different in the ICU, he had decided, first because in some provisional sense the babies belonged to his mother and therefore were related to him, however tangentially, and second, they were usually there long enough to develop and display personalities; unlike the healthy babies, who passed like strangers from the cheery nursery to the bright world practically overnight, the neonates stayed in his mother's unit for weeks or even months. So Connor likes to look at them, these premies and ill infants, though often the prognoses are bleak and his mother seems sad.

Today she's bending over an open isolette, changing a diaper on a tiny thing who mews and coughs and thrashes its arms. "Yes, yes," she tells the baby, "tough little guy, that's good, you're a fighter, you just keep on just like that."

"Is he new?" Connor asks. He's wearing a disposable surgeon's mask they'd given him at the nurses' station, and he keeps his hands clasped behind him.

"Hi, honey," his mom says. "I wasn't expecting you."

"I should have called. Can you go to lunch?"

"If we eat downstairs. Give me five minutes. And yes, he's new. We just got him last night. He's two months premature but I think he's going to be okay."

"What's his name?"

"His last name is Lafferty. He doesn't have any other names yet. They weren't expecting him quite so soon and I think they were still deciding."

"He's sure got a lot of hair."

"Just like a little monkey," his mother coos to the baby. She's adjusting the IV in his tiny foot.

"I'll wait in the hall," Connor says.

They take the elevator to the cafeteria. His mom says she's not all that hungry, so Connor buys her a coffee and a piece of sweet potato pie.

"So I was going through all that stuff you gave me," he says, setting down his tray full of food. "That box of home movies and all those photo albums from the sixties."

His mother says she doesn't know why he's still so obsessed with doing this project, especially since it's too late now. Connor is repressing a thought: if he can finish the film before his father dies, then his father won't die. He's repressing it because he knows if he begins to believe it, it won't be true—and of course that makes no sense whatsoever. Yet in the face of grief, he thinks, there can be defiant gesture. He will press on. He hands his mom a black-and-white photo: his father in fatigues, a military cap, and a bushy fake beard, his mother in a stylish tea-length dress and pillbox hat.

"Halloween 1963," his mom says, hardly glancing at it.

"Tell me that's not what I think it is," Connor says.

"What do you think it is?"

"Your Halloween costumes. Dad was Fidel Castro and you were Jackie Kennedy?"

His mom smiles. "The Department of Philosophy Annual All-Hallow's Eve Costume Masque and Irreverent Symposium. Or something like that. They always had it at Don Zinkler's house—he was the department chairman." She takes a sip of coffee. "Those people were pretty stuffy, David, and I had a lot of fun pulling their chains. I kept hanging all over your dad and calling him 'Castro, mi amor,' and he got into it, too; he kept pinching my behind and leering at me and saying 'Jackie,' only he pronounced it with a Spanish 'j.' 'Whackie, Whackie,' he'd say, 'I love your beeg Nort-American bres.'"

"Good thing Dad had tenure," Connor says, laughing. "But still—Castro with Kennedy's wife! I can't imagine all those egghead profs thinking that was funny."

"It was very funny that night," his mother says. "Three weeks later it wasn't funny at all."

Connor does the math in his head, then nods. She asks if he's going to eat his beets; he pushes his plate toward her.

"That was an awful time," she says. "A lot like 9/11. Everybody glued to the TV, everybody watching this horrible thing over and over again, the funeral, the news reports, Jack Ruby in the police station basement. You just knew that everything was changed, that nothing would be the same ever again." She blinks. "I don't even like to think about it."

Connor watches her slice the beets into bites. He watches the precise movements of her tiny blue-veined hands, bare of jewelry or nail polish. Her white labcoat is spotless. She glances at her watch, then says she still has a few minutes of lunch break left. "Why don't we go up and see him?"

"I hate to see him like this," Connor says uneasily.

"Well, you won't have to much longer."

*   *   *

In the elevator his mother says that she sometimes feels like Humphrey Bogart, and Connor asks her what in the world she's talking about. "You know," his mom says, "that part in *Casablanca* where Rick says 'Of all the gin joints and bars in the world, she has to walk into mine.'" She explains that she has avoided his father for a quarter century, ever since the divorce. Now he has come to her hospital to die.

"Well at least he's not on your floor," Connor says.

His father's room smells of disinfectant and something else Connor can't place at first, something familiar and poignant. He sits by the bed, takes his dad's limp hand and squeezes it. The old man shifts his head slightly. His eyes are closed and he breathes shallowly through his mouth. Thinking of the Castro beard, Connor notices his father has been recently shaved; there's a dried dollop of white foam under one ear and a tiny nick shows on his dimpled chin. Suddenly Connor knows what he's smelling: Old Spice.

He turns to look at his mother. She has opened the blinds, flooding the room with afternoon sunlight, and she's gazing past him, to his father's gleaming clean-shaven face.

"You missed a spot," Connor murmurs.

His mother puts her soft blue eyes on him a moment, then nods to a crystal bowl of yogurt-covered raisins by the bed. "Look what that idiot wife of his brought him. The man is being fed intravenously."

For a while Connor watches a shaft of sunlight shift on the wall above his father's head, thinking *fire, water, atoms, pure numbers.*

Heading out they take the staff elevator; his mother pushes "3," her floor, and then "Lobby," his. They start with a lurch, then slowly go down. He puts his arm around his mom and pulls her close; she takes his hand and Connor feels like weeping with love and sorrow. The elevator numbers light up in green LEDs, 7, 6, 5, 4, like a space-shot countdown.

"Walter Cronkite cried," his mother says suddenly. "Right there on TV in front of the whole world. I do remember that."

River of Time

Time is a river. The ancient Greeks knew that. The perfection of *pi,* the immutable beauty of platonic forms, and time as a river. Connor has been taught these things since childhood. Heraclitus, Pythagoras, Archimedes with his lever. All is flux.

If all is flux, Connor wonders, if you really can't step in the same river twice, if every moment flows irrevocably into the next, if everyone in this bar is drunk and oblivious, then why does it matter whether his sister's guitar is in tune?

But Terri keeps trying, tuning one string, then the next, then back to the first to make some micro-adjustment only she can hear.

"Music of the spheres," Connor mutters. Ptolemy.

He can tell that her B-string is slipping. She can't get it to hold. Flux.

A TV above her head is tuned to a West Coast ballgame, Braves and Dodgers via satellite, closed-caption on, sound down. Connor wonders if Terri has noticed it, if she realizes why half the crowd is staring right past her.

At the set break Connor takes Terri an orange juice. She looks up as he approaches and gives him a wan smile. There's not much of a stage here—just a low platform with a rail on either side—and she's leaning her hip against the rail, tuning up and nodding occasionally at a boyish girl in black who's been bending her ear. Connor can't find an opening, so he stands there holding the plastic cup of OJ listening to a monologue about effects loops and signal chains. Robbie is the girl's name, he finds out later (Connor: "Bobbi?" Terri: "No, *Rob*bie"), and Robbie is suggesting that Terri needs to tweak her sound a little—nothing major, you understand, just cut some of the upper mids, maybe, and rearrange her pedal-board. Robbie critiques the signal chain: from guitar to tuner, tuner to wah-wah pedal, wah to Fuzz-Face, then at last to the amp, a ratty old Peavey that she sneers at.

Connor, adrift, awash in memory, is six years old listening to his father singing: the foot bone connected to the shin bone, the shin bone connected to the knee bone, the knee bone connected to the thigh bone. It's all connected, little buddy. He imagines his father explaining electricity, explaining electromagnetic radiation, explaining the buzzing strings on an electric guitar and the baseball signals from outer space.

"Now me," Robbie is saying, "I prefer fuzz in front, then the wah. You get that more open, rounded vowel sound."

"Wah before fuzz," Terri says, by way of disagreement, but Connor sees she's smiling.

"You should come check us out sometime," Robbie says. "The Lipstick Fix. Four chicks, no guys. We've got a hell of a lead singer."

Terri is wearing extremely low-cut jeans and a halter top, hoop earrings and a tiny glittering stud in her pierced nose. The red and green lights of her electronic tuner flicker as she adjusts her guitar.

"I brought you some juice," Connor finally says, and Terri nods at a black bottle of beer sweating on the railing; "Robbie bought me a drink," she replies, and lifts her eyebrows, waiting for his disapproval: she's had two DWIs in the past fourteen months.

"Terri."

"Yeah?"

"You should drink the juice," he says.

"What are you," Robbie asks, "her daddy or something?"

Her tone is not hostile but not neutral either. "No," Connor says pleasantly, "not her daddy."

"Her boyfriend, then."

Connor gives Terri a little wave and turns back to the bar. Over his shoulder he hears Terri say, "He's my brother."

Death to Unplugged. This is his sister's philosophy. Death to acoustic music. Be electric. Crank it. Scream over it. Rage, rage against the dying of the light. Down with weepy poets hiding behind acoustic guitars.

Connor watches her start the drum machine. She opens this set with an original called "Weapons of Mass Destruction." "Fear," she sings, and holds the note and lets it ring against the distorted guitar, "lies and fear." She rhymes *fear* with *war, destruction* with *deconstruction*. She sings the second line of each chorus in falsetto. It is an odd song, with tonal and lyrical antecedents in an old Black Sabbath tune, "War Pigs."

Someone in the back calls for Buffet, "Margaritaville." It's a joke, Connor thinks, like when smart-asses yell for "Freebird" and mockingly hold lit lighters aloft.

Terri does a Chris Whitley song called "Narcotic Prayer." Desultory applause.

She tunes her low E to a D, tests the tuning, then without irony says into the mic, "This is for the professor—my beautiful blue-eyed dad." She plays a new song, one she just wrote, as yet untitled. Memories and flux and forever-fleeting time. It's a heartbreaking song, Connor thinks, if you listen carefully.

"One for Robbie," she says, and sings:

midnight

two trains collide
everyone dies
everyone dies
it's all over
time is a river

During the second verse the zombie-eyed guys at the bar begin whooping and high-fiving. Without looking up Connor realizes that Atlanta has scored.

Last call. Connor sits at the bar and watches Robbie hitting on his sister. Terri is smiling but shaking her head; after a moment she points toward Connor, who turns away and drains his beer. When he turns back surreptitiously, they're kissing. Connor notes Robbie's hand stroking his sister's hip. The kiss seems to last a long time.

Then Robbie is gone and Terri is counting out the tip jar. Connor helps her coil up cords, case her guitar, take down the mike stand. "Never a dull moment around you," he tells her.

"It was just a kiss."

"She just didn't seem much like your type, Ter."

"I have lots of types."

Connor just shakes his head.

"Anyway, bro', a little kiss never hurt anybody."

"Why were you pointing at me?"

"I told her you were giving me a ride home."

"Good," Connor says.

On the way they hit the drive-thru at Krispy Kreme, *Hot Glazed* flashing in pink and green neon. Though neither is that hungry, family custom dictates that they buy a dozen, a whole box. Terri orders coffee, Connor chocolate milk. Terri says it's ridiculous how many cops sit in the parking lot, and Connor tells her they're just keeping drunks like her off the streets. "Ha," she says, a little wistfully. "Drunk on orange juice."

The road to Terri's takes them through downtown and across the slow river. Connor pulls over on the old iron bridge. They both get out, holding donuts, and stand and peer over the edge into the black water. Then Connor spirals his donut out into space. Terri drops hers directly down. It plops distantly.

"I remember going with him to get donuts before you were born," Connor tells his sister. "Every time we'd cross this bridge he'd pull over and fling one out the window. Every single time."

"Pouring a libation to the gods," Terri murmurs.

"I remember the first time he let me do it," Connor says.

"We should have put him in this river," Terri says. "We could have had a pyre, like they did for Achilles, and slaughtered some oxen, and scattered his ashes off this bridge."

"He'd have liked that."

They get back in the car. They drive another mile without speaking, although Terri touches his shoulder once. Behind them, Connor knows, a different river keeps flowing.

I'm sorry I never got to meet him.

Me too.

He might not have liked me, though.

He'd have loved you.

Yeah? Would he have tried to take me away from you, like he did with Serena?

You never know.

When did he … five years ago, right?

Six years in January.

And after that …

After that, I just … I kind of lost my way for a while. I wasn't right. I went through some stuff, made some bad choices, did a lot of things that … well, let's just say I knew better. Even at the time I knew better. It was stupid. Self-destructive.

Crash and burn.

Yeah, crash and burn. Among other things.

But you're not blaming all that on your dad's death?

No.

Because from what you've told me it doesn't seem like you two were all that close.

We weren't.

But Connor—

I'm not blaming anything on anybody. Just me. I can't really say any more about it than that. You know?

three

Concerning the Wives of Other Men

Five-thirty am. Connor, still half asleep, downshifts and slows, looking for the green mailbox. Suddenly the woman in the seat beside him ducks her head and hisses, "Keep driving." Confused, he half-turns toward her, a woman he has known intimately for just a few hours: "Keep driving," she says again, panicked, dropping her head into his lap. "Shit!" In the dim light of daybreak he sees a black Dodge Ram in her driveway, a man in a reD hoodie sitting on the tailgate. Connor stares straight ahead as he cruises past, neither slow nor fast. "Don," he guesses, resting his hand on the nape of her neck. "What?" she whispers. "Don," Connor says, "didn't you tell me your ex-husband's name was Don?" "No," she says. "Dean. Not Don. My ex-husband is named Dean. This is Jake." In his rearview mirror Connor can see Jake hop down from the truck, standing and staring at Connor's car as it disappears around the curve. "Who in the fuck is Jake?" Connor says.

Not long after his father died Connor found himself trapped in an upstairs bedroom with no way out. The woman he was with had just rolled him over on his back and was kissing his neck, sloppy noisy kisses, dragging her dark hair down his chest and brushing his belly with her big soft breasts, when the front door opened and a man's voice called her name. She leaped up, threw on a robe, and flew downstairs. Connor dressed as quickly and quietly as he could. "You've got someone up there, don't you?" he heard the other man demand, and the woman told him it was none of his business and he didn't own her and what the hell was he doing anyway dropping in unannounced and uninvited, anybody who'd do that deserved whatever he got. Connor stood listening, clutching both his shoes. Heart throbbing, he scanned the room. Under the bed? Into the closet? Behind the door? Nothing appealed. Still holding his shoes, he crept to the window and peered out: fifteen feet into a pink rosebush. He'd survive, but there was no way to raise the window and take down the screen in silence. So he perched on the edge of the bed next to the wet spot they'd left earlier on bottom sheet; it was shaped like a cucumber, he thought distractedly, or maybe more like Lake Erie. He looked back to the bright window. He looked at the framed photo on her dresser: an old couple, her parents, he supposed, holding hands. He reached for his watch and looked at the time and put it on and then he looked at the time again: 2:12 in the afternoon. "And just why the fuck aren't you at work anyway?" he heard her say downstairs. Connor considered his options. Fight or flight. Or just hang tight. Part of him felt he should go downstairs, try to work this out or state his case or make some kind of man-to-man effort at something. Another part said: Connor, this ain't no pissing contest. He wondered what she would want him to do, how not to cramp her style. If he showed without warning, all hell might break loose. On the other hand, he reminded himself, whatever the situation, he was usually able to talk his way out of it. Breathe, Connor. Two slow breaths. His thudding heart calmed. He leaned back on her bed listening to them argue and felt himself getting hard again.

The first time he ever went to bed with a married woman she pulled out an illustrated copy of the *Kama Sutra.* "I thought we might try this," she said, turning pages, "and maybe a little of this, and then...." It took them a few weeks to work their way through the book. On their last afternoon together Connor rested his cheek on her naked hip while she read aloud from a section called "Concerning the Wives of Other Men." "*The wives of other men may be resorted to*," she read tonelessly, "*but the possibility of their acquisition, their fitness for cohabitation, the danger to oneself in uniting with them, and the future effect of these unions, should first of all be examined.*" Desperately sad, Connor kissed her belly button with all the tenderness he could muster. Her eyes drifted shut and she reached to stroke his hair. The book fell to the floor.

In his late twenties Connor briefly dated a woman who bit. In bed she'd cry and moan and bite him anywhere she could reach—his arms, his neck, his chest—and if he pushed her away, she'd bite a pillow or her own arm or hand. Once Connor had her turned face down, hips raised; he was thrusting hard from behind and she had her face in the pillow, shrieking. Without stopping he reached down, braced himself, then suddenly pulled the pillow free. She was shrieking, "Johnny, Johnny, Johnny, oh my God, Johnny," and she kept on even after Connor had finished.

After the first Gulf War he was shooting a TV story about left-behind families and a young wife asked if he would help her make a video love-letter for her husband, who was still in Kuwait City. Connor filmed her slowly stripping out of desert camos down to a red lace camisole; then she kept going, rolling around on her bed in nothing but a pair of red high heels, running her hands over her breasts and whispering to the camera, "This is for you, Sean, I love you, baby, I'm wet for you" and touching herself and licking her fingers and touching herself some more, and when Connor shut the camera down and took a step toward the bed she stopped and said "No," but gently, so he turned away and went back to filming. When they finished she dressed and walked him to the door and tried to give him fifty dollars, which he refused, so she kissed his cheek and thanked him. She never asked for the videotape.

"I'm not going to sleep with you," she said.

"Why not?" Connor asked.

"Because I have a fiancé, and I don't do that. I don't cheat."

"Okay," Connor said.

They started kissing again.

He was twelve and she was eleven, blue eyes and a blonde bob and a hooded blue raincoat, and the other boy who liked her was eleven-and-a-half and he challenged Connor to a fight. *If you don't fight, you're a flat-out pussy.* Connor, who'd been walking away, turned back and started shoving. The other boy got in the first punch—he started swinging as soon as the school bus was out of sight—but Connor, lucky, jabbed him below the ribcage and knocked the breath out of him, then threw him down on the wet pavement, sat on him and pummeled him until the boy gave up. Elated, Connor climbed off: *Who's the pussy now?* and when the broken boy on the ground told him to go to hell, Connor went back and kicked him. The boy started crying. Connor again turned away, talking trash, and the boy again told him to go to hell, so Connor half-heartedly kicked him again. This time when he walked off, he didn't say anything. He just kept walking, head down in the rain. The blonde girl didn't leave with Connor; she didn't even look at him. The last Connor saw of her, she was kneeling beside the boy he'd beaten, touching his face and cooing.

"My husband is a great guy," June said; they were lying under a running shower in a mid-priced motel bathroom, and languid and ravishing, she was soaping Connor between the legs. "He's smart and funny and he helps with the housework sometimes and he makes good money, but God help him, he's a lousy lay. It's quick and efficient and completely mechanical. I knew that about him before we got married, but I kept telling myself there were other things in life and it would be okay. I didn't realize it would matter so damn much."

The Girlfriend Thanksgiving: one year Connor brought home a college girlfriend, and Connor's sister invited *her* girlfriend, and after their father and *his* girlfriend repaired to bed everyone else sat up late drinking wine and flirting. Connor slept with his girlfriend in the guest room and Terri slept with her girlfriend in her bedroom, but at four a.m. in the dark hall Connor, up for a glass of water, bumped into Terri's girlfriend coming back from the bathroom, and without thinking he gently backed her against the wall and kissed her, whispering; she put her hand inside her underpants, touching herself. It took only a minute. She kissed his cheek and slipped away without a word, and Connor, sure he was sleepwalking, stumbled back to bed. In the over-warm room his girlfriend had kicked off the covers; she lay on her tummy with her face turned to one side, breathing softly through her mouth like a little girl. She was wearing one of his old teeshirts and a pair of panties; in the white lozenge of moonlight falling across the bed he looked at her slender white legs and her white panties, and feeling very tender, Connor kissed the top of her head and took her hand.

For a TV news story on the university's annual anthropology conference, Connor was assigned to interview a noted primate behaviorist, a willowy blonde woman in stylish cat-eye glasses. With the camera running, he asked if she could explain baboon mating rituals in terms a typical TV audience would understand—sound bites, simple language, etcetera. The anthropologist gave an ironic smile—if you could even call it a smile, he thought; she just twisted one side of her mouth up—then said, "The male baboon tries to mate with as many females as possible, to insure that his genetic line survives. The female baboon tries to mate with only one male, the one who'll be the best provider for her offspring—except when other males show interest, in which case she mates with them." Intrigued, Connor asked her out after they wrapped. She declined wordlessly, holding up her left hand to show a simple gold band. "That's okay," Connor told her; "it's just a drink." "I don't think so," the anthropologist said. "Why not?" Connor said. She shook her head. "Because I know what 'just a drink' means to men like you."

Betrayal and desperation, guilt and elation. *Sometimes when you're with someone who belongs to someone else....* Connor occasionally starts a thought this way, but it never leads him to anything that applies. Instead he wonders whether he has lived his whole adult life and much of his adolescence with love as his vocation, his passion.

*   *   *

"Hang on a second," Connor said. "Just one thing."

She tried to shush him, moving down his body, undoing his buttons with one hand and hers with the other.

"Seriously," he said. "I always ask. What kind of birth control do you use?"

"Fellatio."

Back in twelfth grade art class they spent a few weeks on contour drawing. The student teacher would put a bunch of bananas or an arrangement of wine glasses on the table and start the class sketching. She was five years older than Connor and she wore batik-print hippie skirts and tight tops and clogs; she'd sit on the desk and swing her legs, smacking a big wad of pink gum, and say, "Draw the *negative* space. Don't draw the *ob*ject. You have to *feel* the space *around* it."

Making love to unfaithful women, Connor feels how their husbands and boyfriends make love, what they do and don't do, what's stale and what's new, what's forbidden and what's comfortable. His lovemaking is a contour drawing built around other men's lovemaking. He's feeling the negative space.

"I've been crazy," Connor sang.

> *I've been a fool.*
> *I've been crazy all my life.*
> *Well I done fell in love*
> *with another man's wife.*

"Sometimes I do think you're crazy," she said.

"That's Muddy Waters," he said. "A Muddy Waters song."

She stood in her sunny kitchen with her back to him,

barefoot in a red robe. Connor came up behind her and put his arms around her and cupped her breasts, one in each hand, and closed his eyes.

"Bliss," he said. "Bliss is what I'm feeling right now. And a little tinge of concern. Just the slightest smidgeon."

She was shucking teabags from their paper envelopes and dropping them into a blue pitcher. She leaned back a bit in his arms, sighing.

Connor experienced a sudden time warp, an almost out-of-body slow-down. He heard a car door slam down the block. He heard the bottom of the tea kettle begin ticking. He heard a blackbird outside the kitchen window. And he heard her say that she couldn't keep doing this, that she wasn't going to do this anymore, that after their tea he was going to have to leave, and not come back.

He had not eaten in two days. He lay in a cold bath, in his cold house, too heartsick to move. *The degrees of intensity of love for the wife of another man,* he read, *are ten in number.* He tried to remember the name of the woman who had left this book on his floor. *1: Love of the eye. 2: Attachment of the mind.* Sharon? *3: Constant reflection. 4: Destruction of sleep.* Sharla? *5: Emaciation of the body.* Not Sharla. *6: Turning away from objects of enjoyment. 7: Removal of shame. 8: Madness.* Shauna. *9: Fainting. 10: Death.* He thought the word "fainting." He thought the word "death." *Thus may a man resort to the wife of another, for the purpose of saving his own life....* Connor closed the book and set it on the edge of the tub. He was shivering in the cold water, his goose-fleshed arms and legs, his shriveled genitals. Dimly he realized he would have to get out soon.

* * *

"Who in the fuck is Jake?" Connor says again. He down-shifts and coasts to a stop sign, checks his rearview: nothing. The woman with her head in his lap has her eyes closed; Connor notes flakes of last night's mascara under her eyes. "I'm screwed," she says. "What in the hell am I going to do now?"

"Do you want me to talk to him?" Connor says, hoping she'll say no.

"Fuck," she wails.

They circle the block. Jake is still standing by his black truck, both hands shoved in baggy hoodie pockets. "What do you want to do?" Connor says. "We can go back to my place."

"If I can just get into the house without a scene. Could you just sit and make sure I get in before you leave?"

They pull into the driveway. Connor starts to unbuckle his seatbelt but she tells him to stay put. She gets out and takes a few steps toward Jake. For a moment it looks as if nothing will happen. Then Jake grabs her wrist and begins shaking her. She goes limp almost immediately.

Connor gets out. "Hey," he yells. "Let her go."

"Go fuck yourself," Jake tells him.

Connor grabs him by the shoulder and tries to turn him around. He sees the red furious face, huge and distorted. Then he's on the ground, gasping: Jake has knuckle-punched him in the solar plexus. When his vision clears he sees Jake is dragging the woman into the house.

Connor pulls himself up. He hears the door slam. At this point he realizes he can do several things. He can knock out a window or try to kick in the door. He can pick up his phone and dial 911. I can even film it, he thinks; if the guy saw me filming him, he'd stop, right? He isn't thinking too clearly. Through the window he can see Jake slinging the woman against the wall, slapping her.

Connor climbs into his car. He starts the engine and guns it. He lays on the horn. When he's pretty sure Jake is looking, he throws his car in gear and crashes it into the back of Jake's beautiful truck. The taillights shatter; the bumper crumples. He backs up to get a running start, hits the horn, and crashes forward again, crushing the tailgate. He backs up a third time. Jake is outside now, screaming; Jake is beating on the roof of Connor's car. Connor ignores him, gunning it again. Connor keeps going. Connor keeps going long after everything around him is wreckage.

Up

Because Felicia is drunk, passed out in the tilted-back passenger seat of Connor's Honda in the Waffle House parking lot; and because Connor is also drunk or not far from it, having just left a New Year's Eve party where at midnight he'd somehow ended up kissing Felicia's best friend's coworker; and because he is carrying his Christmas gift from Felicia, a Sony digital mini-cam, and hasn't yet gotten the hang of it and needs to practice, Connor finds himself directing three raucous waitresses in a kind of home-movie goof-show; it's like a screen test for a bad commercial. Perched on the counter barstools with their backs to Connor, the waitresses wait for his cue, then swing around one after the other and shout: "I'm Wendy!" "I'm Darla!" "I'm Mariposa!"; then "Welcome to the Waffle House!" they scream in unison, falling all over themselves with laughter; so Connor has them rehearse it twice more, letting them get their giggles out, before he tells them that this time is a take: "Put some heart into it, girls; really feel it this time," he says, "and let's see if we can get it in one go; film is expensive" —though it's not film or even videotape he's wasting but bits and bytes easily erased and infinitely re-writeable. The Latina waitress with her dark thick ponytail spins, stretches out one hand like a game-show model gesturing to the grand prize, says again her lilting name; the white girls, one blonde, one blonder, follow suit. In their maroon-and-white striped Waffle House blouses they somehow remind Connor of football referees—which is stupid, he thinks, reframing his shot, not in those brown polyester pants, not with that blue eyeshadow or those limp shag hairdos with their dark roots showing; they're not referees nor anything like, he realizes, but rather something closer to what they actually are, not Waffle House waitresses, quite, but *parodies* of Waffle House waitresses, or perhaps waitresses from Denny's made up to look like Waffle House waitresses, or perhaps not waitresses at all, but rather rejects from the "before" shots on before-and-after TV makeover shows—this is how Connor's thoughts are running as he squints at the flip-up screen of the Sony, the colors vividly oversaturated and grainy, the digital waitresses wheeling 'round and shrieking their welcomes. "Y'all about as stupid as I ever seen you," the cook says, standing at the grill with a scrub brush in her hand, "and Wendy, you get your lazy-ass butt over here and run some dishes" —and Connor shoots this too.

From his booth he can see through the plate glass window to his Honda—in fact, the front of his car is only four or five feet away—and the bright yellow light of the Waffle House sign reflected in his windshield partly obscures his passenger. Connor films her anyway. He is making a Waffle House documentary; he is starting the new year with a visual record of the squalor of his romantic life; he is wishing now that he'd filmed the midnight kiss, that he had filmed every kiss of his life, that he could slump on a sofa somewhere and watch an infinite tape loop of kisses: eyes closed, sigh and tremor, urgency and abandon. What he has instead is snorage, he thinks. Snorage and squalor, and blue-eyeshadowed waitresses.

Mariposa tops off his coffee, slides into the seat across from him. "You sobering up now?" she asks him.

"I'm okay," Connor says.

She inclines her head toward the window. "You shouldn't leave her out there like that."

"Yeah?"

"Yeah."

"She's okay. I'm keeping an eye on her."

"That's not what I meant," Mariposa says. "You treating her bad. It's not worthy of you. It's disrespectful."

"Disrespectful?"

"Look at her out there snoring with her mouth open for all the world to see."

Connor turns his camera on Mariposa. She blinks, rises, brushes the seat of her pants, shakes her head at him. He zooms in on the buttons of her referee blouse.

"You supposed to be her knight," she says.

As he drains his coffee and reaches for his wallet, two Harleys rumble and backfire into the parking lot. Two fat greasy men dismount and enter; from the sissy seat of the second bike a woman slides to the ground, pulls off her helmet, and follows the men in, tossing her hair. "Hey, Leah," Wendy calls to her as she pushes through the door. "Dead woman in the parking lot," Leah says. Like synchronized backup singers, Mariposa and Wendy and Darla all turn and point at Connor.

Leah shakes her finger at him: *You should know better*, and the gesture is somehow so personal, so familiar and intimate, that Connor is certain he knows her. But from where? Leah? he thinks. Leah? She's gorgeous: thick honey-colored hair, wide-set eyes, luminous skin. Connor takes in her outfit: white capri pants and a low-cut white silk sweater, and she's wearing white platforms with tall spike heels, a courageous choice of shoe, he thinks, for the back of a motorcycle. "Hi," Connor says.

"Is that your wife out there?" Leah asks.

"Just my date. She's okay," Connor says, then, helpless to stop himself, he hears himself asking, "Have we met before? I promise I'm not hitting on you. You just look so familiar."

"I hear that all the time," Leah says. "People always think they recognize me."

"Maybe they do. Didn't you used to work at Channel 9? The weekend anchor?"

She shakes her head, smiling, but to Connor it seems more an abstention than a denial. She really is astonishingly beautiful, he thinks, like a supermodel or a movie star. He nods at his camera: "We've been shooting some video. Would you mind if I—"

"Twenty bucks," Leah says. Her unnaturally white smile dazzles him. "I've modeled. I know the going rate. Twenty bucks is cheap."

Connor, feeling an oddly deviant thrill, hands her a twenty and powers up his camera. He steadies his grip, presses RECORD. In the pixilated viewscreen he watches Leah hold the bill up, fold it, then turn her back so he can see her slide it like a slow caress into the hip pocket of her capris. She pirouettes back to face him, making her eyes smile. She touches a finger to her pouty lips, then pushes the finger into her mouth and bites it. She drags her wet finger down her neck, over her left collarbone, and down her arm an inch at a time. She blows the camera a kiss, she waves—*bye bye!*—then she turns and struts to her friends' booth, scooting in beside one of the fat greasy-haired men, laying her lovely head on his leather-jacketed shoulder. Almost simultaneously, two thoughts occur to Connor: one, that he has rarely seen such an incongruous sight, and two, he *did* know her, or at least had seen her before, though not on TV. "I just realized," he says, lowering the Sony. "You're a dancer. You work at Café Risqué."

"Bingo," Leah says. "Now get out of here and go take care of your lady friend. You scumbag bastard."

On the long ride home, Felicia opens her eyes at every redlight. She's not as drunk as she's trying to look, Connor thinks. She won't speak, though, even when he pats her hand and asks how she feels, even when he tells her he's sorry, even when he begins reciting *Where The Wild Things Are* because it's the only poetry he knows by heart, and examining the state in which he finds himself it seems that something by heart is now required. You wear a wolf suit, he tells her. You leave home. You let the wild rumpus begin. You return home. And your supper is still warm. Felicia sighs. "Still motherfucking *warm*," Connor points out, gently poking her with his index finger. "Now tell me, beautiful princess: does that not rot your brain as much as any goddamn knight-in-shining-armor fairy tale?" No response.

They pass a Zip Mart marquee that reads JESUS—DON'T LEAVE EARTH W/OUT HIM. Last week it had proclaimed THE HEART HAS EYES ONLY THE BRAIN KNOWS NOTHING OF, a sentiment that Connor found both mystical and moronic, by turns koan and cliché. He downshifts for a light, shaking his head. A half-mile farther a couple of cop cars are parked side by side for a parley. Because he wouldn't be able to pass a breathalyzer, he straightens up and drives by under the speed limit, staring straight ahead, both hands carefully on the wheel.

I'm sad, Connor thinks, unaccountably sad. Help me. The high road to Felicia's spirals up through laurel and pines, all four-way stops and slow switchbacks. I am filled with remorse, he says to himself a dozen times in a row, and then swinging into the dark driveway he says it aloud: "I am filled with remorse." Maybe if he says it enough it will be true.

Connor finds the house key wrapped inside a $20 bill in Felicia's clutch purse. With considerable effort he's just able to half-carry her into the house and walk her down the long hall to her bed, where she collapses face-down. He rolls her over and starts stripping off her rumpled party duds, tossing everything to the floor. A red sequined jacket. The little black dress. A front-fasten bra, lavender, lacy. Lavender high-cut panties to match. Hoop earrings, a silver hoop bracelet.

Sitting on the edge of the bed Connor drinks a glass of water. He brushes a blonde strand of hair from Felicia's face. He taps the tip of her nipple with one light finger, he bends her brown arms akimbo. She is limp, helpless. Feeling creepy, ashamed, and aroused, Connor, camcorder in hand, begins filming, tracking slowly down the length of her body and back up the other side.

"I'm Mariposa," he murmurs.

If he were really a scumbag bastard, he thinks, he would have left Felicia snoring in the garage. If I were really a scumbag bastard, I would upload this footage and post it on the internet, he thinks.

On the other hand, if he were really a good guy, he'd truly be filled with remorse. If he were really a good guy, Connor knows he'd see himself surrounded by white light, he'd press one button and delete every bit and byte on the camera, he'd make sure to keep her supper warm.

Aloud he says, "On a scale of one to ten, with scumbag bastard being ten…."

He sets the camera aside and starts unbuttoning his shirt. When he's as naked as she is, he lays himself down carefully beside her and closes his eyes in the still world. Just before sleep, he takes her hand. "Are you awake?" he whispers. He whispers her name. Nothing. "Felicia," he whispers, "let the wild rumpus begin."

And then you got married.

Yeah.

Sort of out of nowhere.

Well. It probably looked that way to some people.

Why?

Why did it look that way? Or why did I get married?

The latter. I know why it looked that way. Why did you get married?

I was in love, I guess.

In love. I don't understand that. You were, what? Thirty-eight? Thirty-nine?

Thirty-eight.

And no doubt you'd been in love before, plenty of times—

Yes.

—but somehow you'd never—

True.

So she was different? Better?

Hard to say. I probably thought so at the time.

But now?

But now I think it was more about me than her. I was at a certain point in my life.… I don't mean chronologically. People always talk about their biological clocks ticking, or they say things like "It was just time for me to get married." You know, like you're on a schedule, like you've got it all mapped out. I'm not like that. It was more like … I don't know, sort of a feeling that I'd boxed myself in. That I was caught in this spiral, not a downward spiral, necessarily, but just not going forward. Circling. Stuck. Repeating myself.

Been there, done that?

Well, sort of. I was tired of it all. And I couldn't see any other way to get out of it. You know? This is hindsight, by the way. I wasn't actually thinking all this at the time. All I knew was that I… I could be good. I knew I could. I was tired of being a scumbag bastard.

So you had good intentions.

Yes.

And you followed through on them.

I did. I gave 110 percent.

But in the end it didn't work out.

Obviously.

Don't be touchy. I'm just trying to understand it, to get your side of it down. I want to get it right.

Okay.

Yeah?

Yeah, okay. Sorry.

So it didn't work out. Why not?

Karma, maybe? I'd built up a lot of bad karma.

Do you believe that?

I don't know. Kind of a mechanistic view of the universe, don't you think? But on the other hand, there's an appealing symmetry to it, this idea that what goes around, comes around. You might not believe it rationally, but there seems to be some emotional truth to it.

Payback.

That's one way to think about it.

How long were you married?

A little over two years.

Two Years and Four Months

In the first ten minutes of their first date, a blind date arranged by a mutual friend, Hope asked Connor what he liked to do, and before he could put down his fork she answered her own question: "I bet you're a beach kind of guy, aren't you, beach more than mountains, like you really love long walks on the beach—that's how I am. There's nothing in the world I'd rather do than walk on a moonlit beach." Connor thought Jesus Christ. His mother had once told him to never eat pasta on a first date, but feeling contrary and cranky and reckless—he was tired of trying to make a good impression—he had ordered puttanesca. He picked up his fork again, twirling a few strands of capellini through the sauce, and lifted it thoughtfully. Waiting, Hope raised her eyebrows, blinked twice, nodded at him. Connor chewed. Hope asked, "So you like the beach?" Connor panned around the dim bistro—the Chianti bottle candle-holders caked in rainbows of wax, the framed posters of Napoli and Roma and Mount Etna, the leering waiter—feeling stuck in a stupid movie. Hope smiled.

"No," Connor finally said. He took a deep breath. "I don't like the beach. And I don't think anybody really likes the beach. People who say they do are just being disingenuous. Conceptually the beach is an artificial construct, a kind of layering of travel brochure cliché and romantic associations designed for people oblivious to their surroundings. If people paid attention, they'd hate the beach. I don't like it. I don't like anything about it. I don't like the sand. The sand gets under your contact lenses and in your socks and on the floormats of your car and inside your bathing suit. I don't like the flora and fauna—the odor of rotting fish or the stench of drying seaweed or the way those washed-up jellyfish look—they're grotesque, like internal organs of crashed space aliens or something. I don't like that note of hysteria in the seagull laugh. It reminds me of bag ladies. I don't care for ocean breezes, either—all that humid salt air smelling like diesel fuel and bird guano, making your clothes damp and sticky. I don't like getting sunburned and I don't like getting all greased up with sunblock and I don't like seeing all those overweight middle-aged women in bikinis with their C-section scars exposed or those beer-bellied rednecks in NASCAR caps and baggy swim-shorts with butt-cracks showing. I don't like lying on a blanket on the lumpy sand and listening to whiteboy hip-hop on some idiot's boom box three blankets over. I don't like little kids building sand castles or running along the beach with plastic pails and shovels and I despise seeing dreadlocked Deadheads in their hundred-percent organic tie-dyed beachwear flinging dayglo Frisbees. And it utterly totally creeps me out to watch people body-surf."

About halfway through his speech Hope had set her wineglass down; now she was running a finger over the top buttonhole of her blue blouse, which was unbuttoned three buttons. "Oh my," she said in a pouty bimbo voice—and instantly Connor picked up the irony; he perceived that she was mocking him, that she'd already seen through him, that she knew he'd just been showing off, and because he had underestimated her and she was ahead of him now, he felt his façade crumbling; he felt suddenly and unexpectedly embarrassed and shy and oddly vulnerable. He blushed.

*   *   *

They were married on the beach, of course, barefoot, Connor and Hope both wearing white linen, with her sister as maid of honor and Terri, teary-eyed, as best man. They ignored the mocking seagulls and laughed about the washed-up jellyfish and brought their own boom-box for a bit of background music. Connor had worried he'd have the jitters, or be racked with second thoughts, but he was happily calm—"calm as a hat," he said later—in love and hopeful. I can do this, he told himself; this is a good thing. It will be bliss.

It turned out to be two years of bliss followed by four months of nightmare—suspicion and betrayal, accusations and admissions. On their last night together they made a kind of love that was by turns sad and savage, a fuck of despair and anger and finally tenderness; afterwards Connor coaxed Hope into a bubble bath—lavender and vanilla, her former favorite, with a line of lit tealights burning along the tub's edge. They sat in the steaming water, both facing forward, with Hope in front, and Connor eased her backwards to snuggle against his chest; he wrapped his arms around her, cupping her breasts lightly. Hope sighed. "Don't do that," she said. "You're making this hard enough as it is." Connor let go and began massaging the back of her neck. "I'll never understand this," he said. "Ever."

"David."

"Why did you do it? Just tell me."

"We've gone over this a dozen times already," Hope said. "Talking about it just hurts you more." She squeezed his leg. "And anyway I'm making it easy on you. You should be relieved. You never wanted to be married in the first place. You don't like being married, David, not really."

"You're crazy," Connor said, "yes I do." But he'd hardly slept all week, and now in the warm scented water, after she'd ravished him so thoroughly, he could hardly keep his eyes open; he could not marshal his thoughts or come up with a cogent argument. All he could manage was to repeat "I do."

"You do not." Hope slid down further in the tub, bending one leg and lifting the other to brace against the tile wall. Her head was nestled under Connor's chin; he turned his cheek and laid his face against her hair. Hope said, "You don't like wedding cake. The icing is too sweet."

What? Connor thought. What the—?

"You don't like to go to weddings, even if it's friends of yours. You don't like married people," she said. "They're not cool enough for you. You don't like the kinds of cars they drive and you don't like the clothes they wear or the houses they buy. You don't want children, then all of a sudden you do want them, and then you don't again. You don't like sharing a medicine chest or eating breakfast together or having a joint bank account. You don't like that I make more money than you. You don't like having to ask me if it's okay to change the TV channel, or what color to paint the den, or whether you can go out with Skeet and play pool with a bunch of college girls."

"How is this even relevant?" Connor said, but Hope didn't stop. "You don't like the idea of kissing only one woman the rest of your entire life. You don't like kissing me anymore because of that. Remember all that kissing we used to do? But now I can feel it, you're thinking, This is the last woman I'm allowed to kiss for the rest of my life, and you can't stand it. You don't like being married, David, that's all there is to it. You try, you really do, damn you, but I can tell you're faking it. Give me some credit for knowing you that well, at least."

"This is *bull*shit, Hope," Connor said. "You're *fucking* him. Just admit it."

"I'm in love with him," Hope said. "I'm sorry."

Connor's heart twisted, turned, broke. He felt it.

"Please don't cry," Hope said. "Oh, God, I'm so sorry."

She stood and turned to face him, slinging water, and one of the tealights hissed out.

"Stay," Connor said. "Don't go. Let's not do this, Hope. Please."

But Hope was stepping out of the tub by then, her back to him, reaching for a towel and dripping on the candles. Connor watched them go out, one by one, until there was only one left lit.

Dark-Haired Girl In A Red Pickup Truck

After his marriage broke up, Connor went on a protracted downward spiral, something he described later as his "suicide bomber period," with the emphasis on *suicide.* "It was eight or nine months, I guess, maybe a year," Connor says. "Some kind of kamikaze thing. I was going down and didn't care who I took with me." He used his broken heart to break hearts right and left. He locked up his darkroom with the cameras inside. "What was the point?" Connor missed two deadlines on a corporate training video, and stopped returning calls on his business line. He bounced checks. He ate peanut butter and sardines on stale crackers because he'd stopped grocery shopping. He was drinking a lot, and he'd never been a drinker. He went around numb. Nothing fazed him. "*Suicide* bomber," Connor says now. "I was a zombie."

So. On Halloween he slipped backwards into his black jacket and turned a pair of black vinyl pants inside out and pulled on gray wool gloves with the fingertips cut out, and he powdered his face with cornstarch, pale white, like a geisha's. He began drinking at dusk, fell in with folk who seemed to recognize him, and followed them from one party to another. At some point someone handed him a pink pillowcase stuffed with trick-or-treat candy. Connor ate some and handed some out. "I'm a generous drunk," he said. Various women in costume—hookers, witches, strippers, cats, Playboy bunnies—lent an ear to his tale of woe: he had seen his ex-wife, the former love of his life, cruising around town with a man in a red pickup truck. A ballerina in a blue tutu consoled him, stroking his pale powdered cheek. Later—perhaps at a different party; he wasn't sure—he inserted himself into a discussion of his impaired motor skills. His new friends made him close his eyes and touch his nose; they made him recite tongue twisters; they tried to make him hand over his car keys. "Y'all are haranguing me," Connor said. "Y'all are just a bunch of haranguers." "Dude, you are *not* driving home—do you want to get arrested?" someone said, and Connor thought Why not? He decided there was a certain appeal to being thrown in jail, a temporary and not-unpleasant loss of autonomy, something like an unexpected hospital stay. "Yes," he said. "I do. Where can I get arrested? Arrest me." "Why don't you give me your car keys?" a pretty she-devil asked him sweetly, poking him with her plastic pitchfork. "Why don't you go to hell?" Connor said, and laughed, and couldn't stop laughing. A moment later a sumo wrestler and a fat clown pinned his arms behind him while a harem girl with bare belly riffled through his pants and extracted his keys; Connor cursed them, all three.

"The stupid thing was that I hadn't even driven my car," Connor says, remembering. He had no idea where his car was or at what point he'd starting riding with other people. He doesn't remember leaving the party; one moment he was inside, faces spinning around him, and the next found him out on the dew-damp lawn. Under a buzzing streetlight he threw the sack of candy over his back and headed toward home.

Some indeterminate time later Connor was at a derelict bus stop, standing on the loose lace of his shiny untied shoe and staring at the ragged shards of a broken pumpkin scattered at his feet—some kind of sidewalk augury he couldn't read. He had dredged up a handful of candy corn from the pillowcase with the intent of flinging it at the first red pickup truck he saw, but since no such vehicle had appeared, he had scored direct hits on two substitute targets—a beat-up Buick and a black SUV—and neither had stopped or even slowed down; it was that kind of neighborhood. "Just keep driving," Connor muttered. "How about a little help, damnit? I'm trying to get arrested here."

He fisted some ammo into his mouth, those sharp orange deltoids, like knocked-out jack-o-lantern teeth.

He had just sat down on the bus stop bench when a pickup truck hove into sight. Though it was no more than a vague shape chuffing through the gloaming, Connor knew it was red; it had to be. He stood and dug into his bag, then flung a handful of candy, which rattled off the passing truck like buckshot. "Bastard," Connor shouted.

The pickup stopped. Red taillights popped like flashbulbs; then the white backups snapped on. The truck rolled back ten feet and the right-hand door swung wide.

"Get in," she said.

"Of course I thought it was Hope," Connor says now. "Of course. Why wouldn't I?" The last time he'd seen her, outside her office one afternoon, she'd been climbing into a truck like this; some guy whose face he couldn't see had leaned from the driver's side and opened the door for her and she hopped in and was gone. "So now I'd dreamed her back, come to beg my forgiveness in her new beau's pickup. *Suicide* bomber. I got in. Why wouldn't I?"

He flopped down on the bench seat and looked at the driver: short blonde hair streaked with pink, a glittery pink-and-black eye mask, a pink dress with shimmering wings sewn to the back. On the seat between them lay a magic wand, a crystal rod with a gold star attached.

"Shit," Connor said. "Pardon me."

"For what?" the driver said.

"I thought you were someone else," he said, and he started to get out.

"I probably am someone else," she said. "You need a ride somewhere?"

"It's okay," Connor said. "I'm waiting for a bust." He laughed. "Did I say bust? I mean *bus*. Bus bus bus bus."

"Well, you're in luck. This *is* a bus. Where are you headed?"

"What the hell kind of bus is this?"

"It's a drunk bus. It takes drunks home. Where are you headed?"

"Home?" he said, a little uncertainly.

"Good. Close the door."

Connor thought about it. "Maybe the door stays open," he said. "'Cause maybe I might have to eject on short notice."

The fairy or angel or whatever she was leaned across him and pulled the door shut. The crown of her head bumped his chin and her breast brushed across his biceps. Her scent was citrus and cinnamon. Connor realized he smelled of beer and secondhand smoke. She told him to put on his seatbelt.

"I put it on," Connor says. "I thought about it for a minute and then I did what she told me."

She put the truck in gear. She looked in the rearview, pulled out into the street, then cut her eyes at Connor. Calmly she said, "So just because it's trick-or-treat you think you have the right to crank a bunch of gravel at my truck?"

"I was trying to get arrested," Connor said. Some inner portion of his mind knew how lame this sounded. He scrunched his face up. "It seemed like a good idea at the time," he said.

"Have you ever been arrested?"

"No."

"It's not a good idea," she said, slowing for a stoplight, "at any time."

"Oh," Connor said.

"But if you don't believe me, I can drop you up here at

the police station and we'll see how you like it."

Connor glanced out the window. Two cops were standing on the sidewalk in front of a large well-lit building. "She pulled the truck over," Connor says. "Just pulled it over and rolled down the window and leaned over me again and I was stuck between her and the cops."

"Excuse me, officers," she called.

They ambled over. Connor slumped and looked down.

"Sorry to bother you. I think I need to report a crime."

"What's the trouble?" one cop said, and the other said, "Ma'am?"

"What's the penalty for throwing rocks at moving vehicles?"

"We don't determine penalties, ma'am," the first cop said; "the courts do that," and the second cop said, "Somebody been throwing rocks at your truck?"

She put her hand on Connor's thigh and leaned a little further out his window. "Would you say at least that the vandal would have to spend the night in jail?"

Too late, Connor began to feel that he hadn't been paying enough attention.

"We could arrange that," one of the cops said.

"Is this the guy who did it?" the other cop said.

"This is him."

"Wait," Connor said.

"What's he doing in your truck, ma'am?"

"Turning himself in. I was just giving him a ride."

The first cop shook his head, wiped a hand over his face, and stalked off. The other cop unhooked a Maglite from his belt and shined it on Connor's face. "This lady says you threw a rock at her truck. What's your story?"

"Mistaken identity," Connor ventured.

"Are you drunk?"

Connor shrugged. Demand me nothing, he thought. Just arrest me and get it over with. He blinked stupidly in the bright light. The cop sighed.

"To tell you the truth, ma'am, it's been one of those

nights. We broke up a couple of costume parties that got out of hand and there's been a lot of drunk driving too. I've already arrested eleven people. Now, I can arrest him too but I won't do it unless you agree to press charges. Are you willing to do that?"

Connor held his breath. "Literally," he says now. "It was like everything slowed down right there and then. Like the dashboard clock had gone into super slow-mo, like it had stopped, actually. Like time had frozen. And then I realized something." In that sober still moment he suddenly realized that he *didn't* want to get arrested. "I told myself I'd been a damn idiot."

"Ma'am? Do you want to press charges?"

Connor was watching her face in the dashboard light. He shook his head very slightly, trying to send her a sign. Her magic wand lay glittering on the seat beside him.

"I'll think about it," she said.

"You'll *think* about pressing charges?"

"Sure."

"And what are you going to do in the meantime?"

"Take him home?"

The cop waved them away, disgusted.

They drove a few blocks without speaking. Connor, now strangely lucid, thought he ought to say "thank you," but he also felt he'd been toyed with, that she'd had no intention of getting him arrested. She was just trying to prove a point, he thought, though he couldn't say what that point was. Maybe a power trip thing. He put his feet up on the dashboard.

"Don't do that, please," she said. "You'll scuff the vinyl."

He took his feet down. They were cruising by the hospital now, the halogen-lit parking lot down to a few forlorn cars. The moon was a low sharp scythe just above the horizon. Connor sneezed. "Anyway, it wasn't trucks," he said.

"What wasn't?"

"You said I threw trucks at your rock. But it wasn't trucks. It was candy corn."

"Why candy corn?" she asked.

"Because I was drunk?"

"And why are you drunk?"

Oh hell, Connor thought. He had every right to be drunk, he told her, and he started to explain why. He heard his voice become bitter and maudlin. She listened for a moment, then cut him off: "Man, don't go down that road. You've got to let that go. That's all. You're being childish."

Her tone was gentle, but Connor still felt peeved. "Maybe I have every right to be childish."

"You have every right to be however you want. But why would you want?"

"I just feel like it."

"Stop crying over her, stop thinking she'll come back."

"She might," Connor said.

"Yeah, she might, that's true. But if she does, it won't be the same—you know it won't—so you're a fool to wish for it. What are you supposed to be, anyway?"

Connor was confused. Heartbroken? he thought. Crazed? "What do you mean?"

"What is that costume?"

"Zombie?" he said, not quite sure.

"Zombie? How is that a zombie?"

"I'm a zombie. I just am."

"Zombies eat human flesh. Not candy."

"I wasn't eating candy. I was throwing it."

She stopped for another red light. "Zombie. A lot of people use that word loosely. You know what a zombie is?"

"Tell me."

"A zombie is a body without a soul."

"A corpse."

"Not a corpse. Zombies are alive, or at least animated. They walk around. They can throw candy."

Connor considered this, then, pointing to her getup, asked what she was supposed to be.

"Human flesh, that's what I am. That's what you are too."

She reached up and stripped off her pink and blonde wig, and Connor saw that her real hair was thick and black and lovely in the dim light. She tossed the wig on the dash and said, "A dark-haired girl in a red pickup truck is a sign that even a zombie like you ought to be able to interpret."

Connor mulled it over.

They passed the power station, they rolled by the ruined church, they cruised down the long brown hill and across the river. Connor couldn't understand how she knew where he lived, and said so.

"Because I've been there before."

"You know me?"

"I keep track of zombies, Connor."

To save his life he couldn't think of her name or even remember seeing her before.

"Everything is all confused," he said.

The dark-haired girl pulled up, truck chuffing, to his driveway. "Some advice," she said. "Number one: Never throw anything at anybody's vehicle, especially a vehicle equipped with rifle racks. That's just a dumbass thing to do."

"Yeah," Connor agreed. "Okay."

"Number two: you are not a zombie. You are human flesh. Don't forget that. Now go get some sleep."

"Seems like there ought to be a number three," Connor said.

"Some other night." She nodded toward his house: *go on.*

"Wait a minute. I want you to tell me who you are."

Connor saw her smile in the dashboard light. It seemed for a moment that she might lift her mask, but she didn't. "A friend of a friend," she said, and that was all she'd say.

A couple of dogs—one white, one yellow-orange—broke from the shadows and raced across his moonlit front yard. They streaked by so fast and disappeared so suddenly that Connor couldn't be sure they had really been there. The dark-haired girl leaned across his lap to open his door for him; again he smelled her skin. He asked her if she'd like to come in. She said they both knew it was best if she didn't. "How about lunch tomorrow?" he asked.

"Goodnight," she said.

He groped through his nearly empty pillowcase, then left her with a Hershey's kiss.

four

Depression Glass

The next time Connor saw her it was three weeks later, Thanksgiving weekend, at a gallery opening; she was having her photo taken at the buffet table, posing with a bright strawberry on a toothpick, holding it up like a torch or a lit match. It was the same woman; he was sure of it. She seemed to be waiting for something, maybe for him, he thought, so when the photographer finished Connor made his move. "Don't you drive a red pickup truck?" he asked her.

"David Connor," she said, touching his shoulder, "where have you been? I haven't seen you since Halloween."

He admired the way she rolled with it.

"I think I owe you an apology," he said.

"Accepted," she said.

"I was an ass," he said.

"The head of an ass and the body of a rustic," she said cryptically. "But no harm done. How do you like my prop?" She waved the strawberry in front of his mouth. Connor bent forward and took it in his teeth.

She didn't seem at all surprised that he'd found her. She set the toothpick down and extended her hand. "Sheridan Boudreaux," she said. "My friends call me Boo. And yours call you Connor."

"That's right. Are you ever going to tell me—"

"I know your sister," Boo said, as if that explained everything.

"Ah."

They meandered through the gallery together like old

friends, standing comfortably side by side in front of photos and prints and canvases, and this time she smelled to Connor like vanilla.

"Do you have anything here?" he asked.

"There's a big canvas triptych in the next room," she said, "something from my last project. I saw your super-slow-mo video loop. That motorcycle on the pavement. Is that what you call it? A video loop?"

Connor said that was what you called it, a half-time video loop. He'd finished that piece years ago, he said, but had never shown it. "Did you like it?"

"I liked it," she said. "Usually these video pieces are kind of boringly literal to me. Yours was more abstract. Color and light. Blurry. It had a gestural quality to it, kind of like action painting."

She was small and dark, with shoulder-length dark hair and dark eyes. The other women artists were all making ironic fashion statements—retro hausfrau, thrift-store slut, tie-dyed hippie skirts with clunky combat boots, micro-miniskirts with hightop sneakers—but Boo wore a simple knee-length black dress and black wedge sandals; her arms and legs were bare, and around her neck a piece of amber dangled from a thin leather thong. Connor liked her look and said so.

"Sometimes I feel overdressed at these things," she said, looking around.

Connor, in his usual black jeans and black shirt, extracted a necktie from his black jacket pocket and began putting it on. "To keep you company," he explained. "I always bring a black tie to these things in case I feel underdressed."

"Not to ruin your carefully-chosen color scheme," Boo said, straightening his collar, "but this tie is navy blue."

*   *   *

Two nights later they went out for Thai. Boo drove them in her little white VW. The pickup truck, Connor found out, belonged to her ex-husband; as part of their separation agreement she was allowed to borrow it when she needed to transport oversized canvases. "Also when I need a drunk bus," she added, and he laughed. He asked how long she'd been single and she said "Not long enough" and Connor said he knew what she meant. "By the way," she said, "in case you're wondering, my ex is living with his old high school girlfriend. He's not seeing your ex. I checked." "It hadn't occurred to me," Connor said; "I guess it's a big town," and Boo said "Yes, and there are lots of red pickup trucks." Between the Goong Yang and the Tamarind Duck, she told a complicated story about one of her paintings, a provocatively posed full-frontal nude self-portrait that incited in her former spouse an insane jealousy. While she described the canvas—a hand mirror, two orchids, a string of pearls, reds and golds and skin-tones—Connor watched her hands: she tugged at one of her dangly earrings, she drew shapes in the air, she placed her palm over her heart, she laced and unlaced her long fingers, all apparently without realizing it. "I want to see it," he told her, "this painting." "You can't," Boo said: her ex had slashed it to shreds with a utility knife. "I had an opening coming up and he didn't want me to show it, didn't want other people looking at me. So he destroyed it. Some twisted variation on *If I can't have her, nobody else will.*"

"That's pretty sick," Connor said.

"Sick was sort of our middle name," Boo offered. "But I didn't mean to get started on that. Tell me what you're working on."

He was between things, Connor said. "In the mean-time I volunteer for clinical trials, just to keep a little cash coming in. I'm doing one right now where they needed a nonsmoking control group."

"For what?" Boo asked, and Connor said he didn't know; he just showed up and did what they wanted and took their money.

Over Boo's shoulder he could see the restaurant owner, a tiny Asian woman—Laotian? Cambodian? he couldn't remember—breastfeeding a baby behind a carved teak screen. "What are you looking at?" Boo wanted to know, and Connor told her, hoping he didn't sound like a pervert. "Babies seem to be following me around lately," he said; "They're everywhere, all right," Boo said, a bit sourly, Connor thought, and then, abruptly, she said, "I know it's kind of early but would you like to skip the movie and go back to my place?"

She lived on the second floor of a 1930s bungalow. "We're renting out the bottom," she said, reaching for his hand to lead him up the steep stairs; Connor noted the "we" but didn't ask. Inside, while he admired her windowsill collections of blue bottles—"mostly they're Depression glass but I do have some newer pieces," Boo said—she lit candles and put on a CD: a stoned swirl of guitar and hyper-manic drumming, then a light, almost ethereal voice floating in above the frenzy. "Wow, Jimi Hendrix," Connor said, "that's unusual. For a girl."

"I get that from my mom," Boo said. "I love Jimi Hendrix. Of course I wasn't even born when he died—you know he was only 27?—but my God, this music is timeless, really." She had an extensive collection of bootlegged concerts, she said, and when she was painting she'd put "Little Wing" or "Axis: Bold as Love" on infinite repeat and listen to them nonstop for a couple of hours at high volume; she told him she liked to have sex to "Machine Gun" from *Band of Gypsies*. She was standing by the stereo when she said this, and Connor hesitated only a moment, then took three steps toward her, trying to read her expression. She reached out and rested her hand on his hip. They kissed, Connor bending to her upturned face. They kissed a long time and when she finally broke away, both of them breathless, she told him he had to leave. "What?" Connor said, "you're kidding, right?" "No," Boo said, "you have to leave right now. Either that, or go sit in the bean bag chair by yourself." Connor thought this was so funny that he did it; he sat in the stupid blue bean bag chair, smiling at Boo and feeling, for the first time in months, something like happiness.

Eventually things progressed. Eventually they went to bed. "Good God," Connor said after, when he could speak, "now *that* was chemistry," and Boo, who'd collapsed on top of him in a flurry of fluttering kisses, murmured into the hollow of his neck something that sounded like *yes*. Like *yes yes yes*.

Her studio room was in chaos—scraps of canvas and paper littering the floor, brushes and ink pots and easels and bottles of colored liquids, discarded tubes of paint, an old computer cycling through its screen-saver, a slide projector aimed at a white wall, a small color copier blinking on standby. On a square scrap of slate blackboard hanging by the door was a scrawled title: *The Donna Project*. Because there was an order to it, Boo explained, a narrative, she took Connor's hand and walked him through it, piece by piece. Some of the pieces were mixed media, framed assemblages of drawings and photographs—a teen-aged Donna, Donna as a child, Donna's baby pictures—augmented with acrylic and crayon and typed-up printed-out diary entries. Others were paintings, including two life-sized nudes of a middle-aged Donna with the breasts rendered full and heavy. Connor stood for a while, admiring Boo's work—there was a homey, honest quality to it, he thought, the slight slackness of the woman's body, the smile lines and stretch marks and the brown mole on her belly—then moved to the next piece, which on a dark background depicted Donna with her chest bound in gleaming white bandages. Connor took a sharp breath, guessing, and Boo squeezed his hand. He could hardly look at the final painting: Donna, bare-chested, with her head bowed over the fearful dark scars. Connor looked and looked, then dropped Boo's hand and walked through the project a second time. The work was raw, intense; she had tapped the fear and grief, and something beyond that as well, some other emotion churning to come through. He felt it, rather than thinking it; he felt horror and hopelessness and sorrow somehow in the very brushstrokes.

"Donna is a friend?" he asked softly.

"Donna was my mother," Boo told him.

After a moment Connor said he was sorry and that it must have been so difficult, separating the life from the art.

"Life *is* Art, Connor. I don't really separate it," Boo said. "And neither do you." He put his arms around her and pulled her close. "Finish the film about your father," Boo whispered.

"I hate you, David," his sister said to him at the cafeteria two weeks later.

"Why do you hate me, Terri? What have I done now?" Connor said, slicing his beets.

"I hate you because you're happy and I'm miserable," she said.

"I'm happy?" Connor asked. He thought about it and decided that yes, he was happy. He said it again: "I'm happy."

Terri nodded. "Any idiot could see that," she said. "You're in love."

In love. It was that simple, he thought. "Yes."

"And this time it's different."

"It feels that way. Yeah."

"I vaguely remember her from high school. She went by Sheri then, not Boo. After graduation I probably didn't see her for ten years. Then I bumped into her last April and she asked about you."

"You didn't tell me."

"It just slipped my mind. Anyway, what's so great about her?" Teri asked, and Connor wondered if she were jealous.

"She's smart," he said. "She's sassy and funny. She's got style. She looks really hot in my underwear."

"Little too much informa—"

"—And she's good for me. She's a lot better artist than I am. She makes me up my game. Now why are you miserable?"

Terri took a bite of seven-bean salad, made a face, reached for the salt. "I'm lonely," she said. "And I want to have a baby."

"You what?" Connor said, staring at her. He let a forkful of meatloaf fall into his turnip greens.

"You heard me. I want a baby. But it doesn't look like that's in the cards for me."

"I'm assuming you've ruled out actual intercourse."

"With a man? Correct."

Connor considered. It wasn't impossible, after all. "Well, I mean, you could always find a sperm donor and make a tur—"

"—don't use that phrase, David, I hate that term, damn it. Imagine growing up knowing that your mom—"

"—used a turkey baster to—"

"David, damn it."

"Okay, okay, I'm sorry." He reached across the table, squeezed her hand. "But hey, I'm sure you could figure out something—"

"Can we not talk about it right now?" Terri asked him.

"Sure. Sorry."

His sister nodded. Then she told him, "I'm just gonna say one more thing about this."

"What's that?"

"I'm gonna kill you if you guys have a baby before I do."

Connor wondered what he wanted. He had a dream in which Terri loaned him a baby, a little girl, and he was showing her how to blow bubbles with a wad of gum. Then while his back was turned the baby got into his darkroom, bent on drinking the chemicals. (This was when he realized it was a dream: he shot digital; he hadn't had a darkroom for a decade.) Connor told the baby, No No No, we don't drink chemicals, and the baby laughed and said that Terri—she said "Terri"—let her drink all the chemicals she wanted, and then Connor woke up.

There seemed to be babies everywhere. In magazines, on the television, at the playground and the mall, in the waiting rooms at the med school. They were slung in snuggies like little papooses, just a tiny face peeking out. They were invisible in car seats, their mothers looking in the rearview and making goo-goo faces. How had he not noticed? Of course he'd noticed. Why was he noticing now, what was different? Something had changed, he told himself.

But it seemed Boo didn't want to talk about it.

They were lying half-dressed on her sofa. They'd just finished watching a film about Lee Krasner and Jackson Pollack—a bitter, cynical love story fueled by alcohol and cruelty and brilliant art—and hesitantly, feeling he might be heading down a tortuous pathway, Connor ventured the thought that they might have been happier if they'd had kids.

"They were artists," Boo said, "they weren't supposed to be happy." She nibbled on Connor's collarbone. "That's a joke, by the way."

"Ha ha. But still...."

"Lee Krasner didn't need to have kids," Boo said. "She had Jackson. He was kid enough for her. And as far as him being any kind of father—can you imagine Jackson Pollack changing a dirty diaper? Or even giving a baby a bottle?"

"Not much help," Connor agreed.

They lay quietly a moment, listening to the kitchen clock ticking, the fridge icemaker refilling. Then Boo said, "What is it?"

Connor kissed the top of her head. "I guess Terri's got me thinking about kids," he said slowly. "About having a baby."

Boo shifted her weight, turned her face toward the ceiling. "You'd make a good dad."

"And you a good mom."

"A good mom," Boo repeated. She seemed sad.

"Why not, Boo?" Connor asked. "You're not too old. You're thirty-six. Lots of women have kids in their thirties, even in their forties. My mom works in natal care and she sees it all the time."

"It's not an age thing."

"So you just don't want kids? At all? You've never wanted a baby?"

"It's not a matter of what I want."

"What do you mean?"

Boo was shaking her head.

"I can't have kids, Connor. I'm preeclamptic. Do you know what preeclampsia is?"

She'd been pregnant once, twenty-three and single and pregnant, she told him, and that's how she found out. "There are two cures for it," Boo said, "delivery or abortion. There's no known prevention except to not get pregnant again."

"You were pregnant?" Connor said, trying to catch up.

"Yes. That's how I found out. This is a condition that you don't even know you have until you actually get pregnant. Nobody knows what causes it. Hypoxic placenta. Autoimmune disorder. Vascular dysfunction. Or something else entirely, or a combination of things. The bottom line is that it's a life-threatening condition for the mother. So I'm not planning on getting pregnant again." She sat up and turned her back to him. "So you need to be sure you're not wasting your time with me. You might need to be with somebody who can give you kids."

Connor sat up too, leaned to look at her face. He thought she might be crying, but she wasn't.

"Boo," he said, "it's okay. First, I don't even know, really, whether I want kids. So I don't feel like I'm wasting my time with you. And second, that was a long time ago, your pregnancy, what, fifteen years? By now there's probably some kind of treatment, don't you think, a new procedure or something, you know? If you really wanted to have kids, you could probably—"

Boo closed both eyes.

"Well, anyway," Connor said, "the bottom line is that we shouldn't make it an issue. Let's not, okay?"

"But it is an issue. I can tell. I can tell it's going to be an issue for you. Be honest. You want a baby."

"No, no, no," Connor said. "I was just thinking about it, that's all. It's not going to be an issue, Boo. Trust me."

"I want some water," Boo said. She got up. "Do you want anything?"

"I'm good," Connor said, watching her walk away. He stood. "I'm sorry I upset you, baby."

From the kitchen she called, "I'm not upset." He listened to her opening the fridge, pouring water from her blue pitcher. Then she said, "But as long as we're talking…." She reappeared in the kitchen archway holding a half-full glass. "There's something I need to tell you, and I don't think you're going to like it. But you're just going to have to trust me. And don't get mad, okay?"

Connor sat back down on her sofa.

In the dream Connor and Boo were driving somewhere in an old red convertible, Connor at the wheel. He asked her if it was too windy, if she wanted to stop and put the top up. Boo threw her hair back into a ponytail. "I like it," she said. "I like wind in my face. Drive faster." Connor didn't know about that. He glanced down for the speedometer but before he could read it, he felt the car running off the road and he jerked his eyes back up. This happened twice more, with Connor getting more and more anxious. "I don't really know where I'm going," he said, and Boo turned up the radio and started shimmying in place. They passed a hitchhiking baby, a toddler standing beside a blue car seat with his thumb out; Connor started to pull over but Boo stopped him. "Keep driving," she said, easing herself across the bench seat to lay face up in Connor's lap. Connor watched the baby recede in his rearview. "Stomp on it, love," Boo said, unbuttoning her blouse, cupping her bare breasts in both hands, kissing Connor through his pants, "let's kick it up a notch," and Connor, gazing at her hard nipples, her lips, her eyes, stomped on it and kicked it up a notch and ran them off the road and over a cliff, and falling, thrashing, woke up hard and lonesome.

He hadn't seen her or heard from her in eight days. So that was that, he thought. At first he figured everything would blow over, that they just needed some space, that they'd be back together after a weekend apart. But Monday came, then Tuesday, then he picked up his phone and texted *you ok?* He waited two days for an answer and then told himself to forget it. The next day while vacuuming under his bed he found a silver hoop earring that he thought must be hers; he didn't remember Boo wearing hoops but neither could he think whom else it might belong to. He took a photo of it and attached the photo to an email and typed her address in the "to" line and then thought better of it and deleted it. He emailed Hope instead, asking if she wanted to have lunch, and within an hour she emailed back, saying she was surprised to hear from him and asking for a raincheck, and saying that she hoped he would have a happy birthday. Connor hadn't thought of it. At midnight he'd turn forty-one, he realized, which for some reason sounded worse to him than forty.

Because he didn't want to spend his birthday alone, he ended up having dinner with his mother, who, rather than taking him out, cooked his boyhood favorite: a chicken-and-cream-of-mushroom-soup casserole that Connor had not thought about in years. His mother looked tired, he noticed. She'd pulled a double shift at the neonatal unit the day before and was still recovering, she said. Connor said he felt bad about making her cook, but she said a casserole wasn't really cooking—just throw some stuff in a baking dish. "Besides, it's your birthday," she said. She'd gotten him a presents, too: an oversized hardcover edition of the photographs of Ralph Eugene Meatyard ("I know you love him." "I do, I do! How did you know?") and a soft black leather dopp kit, double-zippered, elegant and masculine. "It's beautiful," Connor said, holding it up to his cheek. "There's something inside, too," his mother told him, and Connor unzipped the bag and pulled from a nest of pale blue tissue paper a small cobalt blue bottle. "It's Depression glass," his mom said. "I remember that Boo collects blue bottles, and I thought maybe you two could share it, you know, if you decide to set up housekeeping together—"

Depression glass, Connor thought. Perfect. Aloud he said, "Boo and I aren't seeing each other anymore."

"You're not?"

Connor shook his head.

"Oh, David. I'm sorry. I had high hopes for you two. What happened?"

"We had a big disagreement about something."

His mother raised an eyebrow.

"Her ex-husband had been living with his new girlfriend, but last week they had some kind of blow-up and she threw him out and he needed a place to stay. So he moved back in with Boo. She said it was just going to be for a couple of days, just until he found a new place, and that she told him he'd have to sleep on the couch, but I had a little trouble visualizing that. They've only been separated six months."

"Why couldn't he stay in a motel?"

"I don't know. They still have joint ownership of the house. I guess he feels like it's still half his."

"I see your concern. I wouldn't like it either. But it comes down to a matter of trust, doesn't it? You don't trust her, David?"

"It's not that," Connor said. "It's not that I don't...." He saw his mother shaking her head sadly. "Well, yeah. Okay. I guess it's a trust thing. Yeah. So I lost my temper and walked out, and I haven't heard from her since."

"When was this?"

"Nine days ago. I kept expecting her to call or text or something, but she hasn't, which tells me that he's still there. So...." Connor shrugged.

They cleaned the kitchen together, Connor rinsing and his mother loading the dishwasher and putting away leftovers, scraping half-eaten birthday cake down the disposal. "Forty-one years," his mother said. Connor, knowing it had been a difficult delivery, asked if he'd been a lot of trouble, and his mother told him he was the best baby ever. "Once you got here you were no trouble at all," she said; "you were always laughing, always happy." "Huh," Connor said, "wonder what happened to me?"

As he was leaving his mother asked what he planned to do about Boo. "Nothing," Connor said. "I guess I just have to let her go."

In the dim hallway, his mom seemed sad. She flicked on a light. "It's none of my business, I know," she told him. "But I just want say something, and then I'll shut up."

"Say it," Connor said.

"You need to try harder. You give up too easy."

No I don't, Connor thought.

But on his way home, wondering if she were right, he detoured thorough Boo's neighborhood, telling himself that he just wanted to see if there was a red pickup truck in her driveway. There wasn't, and her living room light was on. Not thinking, Connor pulled in. What to do? He thumb-typed a text—*im downstairs im coming up*—then sat looking at his phone. He backspaced and inserted an ampersand and two apostrophes, reread his message, put the phone down, looked up at her lighted window. Fuck this, he thought. He put the car in reverse, sat a moment, sighed, then put it back in park. He picked up the phone. He hit SEND.

"It's my birthday," he said when she opened the door. "I'm forty-one years old."

Boo was barefoot and sleepy-eyed. She had her hair pulled back in a ponytail, like in his dream; and she was wearing a thin white teeshirt, through which Connor could see her breasts, and a pair of black boxer shorts he recognized as his.

"Happy birthday," she said.

"I brought you some Depression glass," he said, handing her the bottle.

Boo looked at it for a moment, turning it in her hands, holding it up to the hallway light shining behind him. "This isn't Depression glass," she said. "It's Elegant glass. A lot of people get them mixed up. They're from the same era but Elegant glass is better. It's handmade and the color is deeper and shinier. This is beautiful, Connor. Thank you."

"Boo," Connor said, "baby," he said, voice cracking, and then he couldn't say anything else except that he was sorry. She searched his face slowly, then said it too, and she said she missed him. He touched her cheek, her hair. Then they were kissing, tentatively, carefully, and Connor's heart shifted, released, settled in and knew home. And when Boo broke the kiss she whispered, "I want to paint you."

And that was how Connor became a Project.

Blue Blue Windows

Connor was standing under the Plexiglas shelter with his video camera, waiting for a city bus. He wasn't planning to ride—his car was parked a block away in a vacant lot—he just wanted to film the bus windows. Boo had told him the color of bus windows at night was incredibly blue, like swimming pool water lit from below, that there was an unearthly glow in bus windows, something that couldn't be captured on film, and Connor thought that might be worth checking out. He had to admit that he'd never really noticed the color. It was his sort of image but somehow he'd overlooked it. He leaned against the side of the shelter and shot down the avenue, into oncoming headlights.

A Latino man in baggy Army fatigues was watching him. He rubbed both hands over his face, smiling, then said, "You don't ride this bus much, do you, bro?"

"Not much," Connor admitted. "Why?"

"Why? 'Cause you're carrying that nice piece of equipment. Good chance for somebody to relieve you of the responsibility of that thing."

"On the bus?"

"On the bus or near the bus."

Connor looked at him, trying to read his intent. The man's dark eyes were in the shadows but he was still smiling. Connor said, "I wasn't really planning on getting on the bus. I'm just shooting some pictures of the bus."

"I tell you what, man. There's nothing interesting 'bout this bus. You want to see some picturesque buses, you go to Guatemala. Buses there worth shooting."

"Yeah?" Connor said. "You from Guatemala?"

"Hell no," the man said. "I'm from Mexico. Hell with Guatemala. You know? Everything in Guatemala is like a million years old. You visualize that? A bus that's a million years old! Ha! That's something worth shooting."

Over the years Connor had learned that the universe was constantly sending him subjects. He had trained himself to pay attention, to accept a gift, to go with serendipity. Now he turned his camera slightly, wondering aloud if he might ask a few questions. The man shrugged, then nodded.

"What else about the buses," Connor said.

"You know Bondo? What it is?" the man asked.

"Tell me."

"Bondo. Some kind of plastic. Like mud for dents. Auto body work. Fills in dents. It's this shitty gray color, big gob of dried junk. My friend, every car in Guatemala is held together with Bondo."

Connor laughed, holding the camera steady.

"And the cars, and buses, and trucks, and scooters, man—all the colors of the rainbow. All the colors of the freakin' world, man. Every color you can get with cheap spray-paint. Yellow! Just ugly, man, like hippies painted everything. And what do you call it, words and letters backwards and all this—" He reached into the air holding an imaginary spray can, swooping his hand in loops and slashes. "What is that, man?"

Connor took a stab at it. "Graffiti?"

"Yes. Graffiti. Done by vandals. Every thing in G-City, man, every *thing* you see anywhere, is covered with graffiti. Do you know what I'm saying? The buses there, they have a hundred words, a thousand. All written by vandals. Words that make no sense. Letters that spell nothing. And all the paint peeling off, raining all the time, rot, tropical crap, man, awful place, Guatemala City, freakin' Maya steal everything you got."

A cop car came flying by, blue lights flashing. Connor followed it with the camera until it was out of sight, then turned back to his interview. "You call them Maya?" he asked.

"Guatemalans, sure. Mostly they're *indios*, you know. Maya ancestors. You know Maya? Pyramids, the temples, cities in the jungle? You know? Very mysterious people, man. By the way, my name is Roberto Morales." He spoke to the camera and gave a brief bow of his head.

"David Connor," Connor said, offering his hand; Roberto shook it, repeating Connor's name gravely. "So if you're Mexican, what were you doing there?" Connor asked. "In Guatemala?"

"Oh, man, I was stupid in love with some woman. A Maya woman. I go see her all the time. Five hundred miles! How many women you think are in Mexico? You don't know. Guess. How many?"

Connor, with no idea whatsoever, guessed fifty million.

"My friend, you are correct. Fifty million."

"Really?" Connor said, laughing.

"Fifty million Mexican women I could fall in love with. But that is not how it happens for me—not with a Mexican woman. For me, Guatemala. Ten years of my life. Going there every opportunity. On a bus, sixteen hours from Matamoras to G-City. Twice a month. Insane, man."

"Must have been something special about this woman," Connor said.

"Oh man, you just don't know. Can't be put in words, this thing."

In the brief silence Connor felt a sudden sadness. Roberto looked down at the sidewalk, then back to the camera; he wiped his mouth with the back of his hand, shaking his head. He sighed. Connor lowered the camera and waited. After a moment Roberto asked if Connor were married.

"I have a girlfriend," Connor said.

"She's pretty, I bet. What's her name?"

"Sheridan Boudreaux. Her friends call her Boo. And yes, she's very pretty. And smart."

"You love her, Davíd? You always thinking about her?"

Connor said he did, and he was. He said he had looked for Boo a long time, his whole life, in fact.

Roberto lifted one shoulder, smiling. "You take care of that, then," he said. "Just my advice, amigo."

"Thanks," Connor said.

With two fingers Roberto pulled a pack of cigarettes from his shirt pocket; he offered the pack to Connor, who shook his head.

"So what happened to your woman?" Connor said. "Your Guatemalan girlfriend."

Roberto tucked the cigarettes back into his pocket. "Long story, and you don't have time to hear it or me to tell it."

"I'm not going anywhere."

"Too late now," Roberto said. He pointed down the block, where the traffic light had changed and a big city bus had wheeled around the corner, heading toward them. "Maybe another time."

"When?" Connor said. "I make films. I'd like to film your story. When can we talk again?"

"I'm on this bus every night, man. But it's not so interesting, that story. Not such a good movie. Now Guatemala, man, eh? Crazy shit down there. Got to go down there someday, film some of *that* shit."

Connor said he would like to do that.

"Seriously," Roberto said. "This"—he waved at the bus pulling to the curb—"it's nothing. You want to shoot buses, go to Guatemala. Go soon, okay?"

"Okay."

"Guatemala," Roberto said.

"Yeah," Connor said.

Connor turned his camera back on and shot Roberto climbing into the bus. Then he stepped a few feet back and crouched to get a wide angle on the windows. He filmed for a few seconds before he noticed. The windows weren't blue at all. They were transparent, like aquarium glass, just ordinary windows lit from inside with white fluorescent light.

Boo had a bad migraine. She'd had it all day, she told Connor on the phone, and hadn't been able to eat or work or do anything except "lay up in the bed," as she called it, with her sleep blindfold on, but all of a sudden she was ravenous. "Say what you want and I'll have it there in half an hour," Connor told her. "And I'll rub your shoulders too."

He loved Boo wildly, in a way that made his stomach hurt when they were apart. And he loved her in a nurturing, steady way too that was new to him. She was quirky and funny and strong-willed, easily able to fend for herself, but more than anything Connor felt compelled to protect and care for her. He realized he was doting on her in a way that might quickly become annoying, but couldn't seem to help himself; endorphins were involved, he thought, some kind of feel-good chemical blasting through his bloodstream when he brought her flowers or brushed her hair or cooked her a meal.

He pulled into a drive-thru and ordered her salad—blackened chicken strips, no tomatoes—and an unsweetened tea. The voice on the box asked if he needed any sweetener with that. "It's for my girlfriend," he said, not caring that it made no sense.

At Boo's house he let himself in, arms loaded with his video gear and the takeout salad. "In here," Boo called from the bathroom; she was soaking in a bubble bath with a washcloth over her eyes. Connor put down his packages, knelt and kissed her wet forehead.

"How you feeling, baby?"

Boo just smiled and nodded.

"I got your salad and an iced tea. Ready when you are."

"You're so sweet, Connor. Thank you. I'll be out in a few. Did you eat?"

"I'm okay."

"You should eat. Have some of mine. We'll share."

In the kitchen Connor divided the salad between two plates and poured himself a glass of water. He set the table, lighting the candles and dimming the overhead. In a minute Boo appeared in blue pajamas, her damp dark hair wrapped in a crimson towel. Connor gave her a kiss.

"You smell good," he said.

"I feel like warmed-over hell," she said, picking a piece of chicken out of the salad, "but maybe this will help. What have you been doing, love?"

Connor told her about the bus windows, how they were nothing special, and Boo said it must have been the wrong kind of bus; she was sure the windows on the bus she'd seen were blue. "I'll keep looking," Connor said, and then he told her about Roberto Morales and his Guatemalan girlfriend. He watched to see if Boo found the story funny, but he couldn't read her face in the candlelight. When he was finished she said, "I love how people just open up to you. You've got a gift, Connor."

"It's not me. It's the camera. The camera loosens them up. It's kind of crazy what people will say and do if you're filming them. Anyway, I brought it along if you want to watch some later."

Boo smiled. "Set it up."

"You must be feeling better."

"Yeah. A little bit. You can still rub my shoulders, though."

They finished their salads and Connor took the plates to the kitchen. While Boo was combing out her hair, he wiped down the table and blew out the candles. He plugged the video camera into her TV and backed it up to the start of his interview with Roberto. "Here it is," he called to Boo.

They sat on her sofa holding hands.

The image was grainy—"low light," Connor said, "but it's usable"—and a bit shaky in spots, but the audio was good. Roberto described the Guatemalan buses; Roberto explained about his girlfriend; Roberto claimed there were 50 million women in Mexico. Boo and Connor laughed, and Connor kissed the side of her face, feeling her smile crinkle under his mouth. He heard himself say on the video *Must have been something special about this woman,* and heard Roberto reply, *Oh man, you just don't know. Can't be put in words, this thing.* And then there was a pause, three, maybe four seconds. "Oh wow," Boo said.

"You feel it too?" Connor asked.

"Right there," she said. "Like the whole tone just shifted."

"Yeah. Got real all of a sudden."

"Wow, Connor. Back that up, would you? That's a real moment. That's something. You need to do something with that. Seriously."

Connor had a Neil Young song going on his car stereo and he was singing along. *Blue blue windows behind the stars.* He ran a red light, following too close behind a city bus. *Yellow moon on the rise.* He punched the back button and started the track over. The bus turned left and Connor kept going straight. He told himself he was *helpless helpless helpless,* but he didn't really believe it.

Three nights running he went back to the bus stop, but no Roberto. He bought some tokens and rode the whole route, showing his grainy video to the regulars. No one admitted to knowing the man he had filmed. He tried directory assistance, the white pages online, Google. Roberto Morales was an obstetrician in Tampa, a jazz musician in California, and a Guatemalan novelist known for his magical realism. "That's pretty bizarre,"

Boo said when he told her. "Like he's a character in one of his own stories, just magically appearing in a bus stop a thousand miles from home…."

"Or more likely, just a guy who's read Roberto Morales and is having a little fun with the ignorant gringo."

"Like if I went around South America introducing myself as Judy Chicago."

"Or Lee Krasner," Connor said. "Yeah, maybe."

He kept coming back to that moment in the video, the little pause, the caesura where the mask slipped. Some of the time he felt it, the sadness, the sense that he'd gotten past a public persona and down to flesh and bone and heart and spirit. Other times he looked and looked and couldn't see it. It was just an awkward pause, a break. He wondered what to do.

"You're wise, Boo," he said. "You've done a lot of pieces like this, things based on people. Advise me."

He was standing nude in her studio room, hip cocked slightly sideways, face in profile, a sunlit open window behind him. It was to be the first of four nudes she had envisioned, and she kept a tape recorder running while she painted, in case he said anything that might be useful for her documentation.

"There's not much I can advise you on here, Connor. You just see the emotion, the heart, and go for it. Emotion is fleeting. You have to grab it. Try to get it on the canvas, on film, in the clay, in the words, whatever's the medium. You don't want it to get too cerebral, right? Keep it heart-first."

She was barefoot, wearing a sleeveless white undershirt and a gray pair of Connor's boxers. She had a smudge of green paint on her elbow and two more on her inner arm, and Connor loved her, loved looking at her face while she worked, how she focused, how she glanced back and forth between him and the canvas, how she wielded her brush so surely.

"You get to a point where you control the medium,"

Connor said, "where you have technical ability to do pretty much whatever you need to do. But the content, now that—"

"No, baby, you're missing my point," Boo said. "It's not about technique or medium or any of that. It's about how much that man loved his girlfriend. It's about how there weren't any words for it. He couldn't get it across to you, or to anybody else. He couldn't tell it. You just have to see it, to feel it. You know, there's not much use talking about it. It's just there."

Connor shifted his weight a little, then went back to the pose.

The last time he rode the Morales route, as he'd come to think of it, the bus was almost empty. Connor scanned the passengers' faces, seeing no one familiar. He sat up front, just behind the driver, a tall Black man who balanced his blue cap on one knee as he drove. Connor asked if he'd seen Morales lately.

"You still looking to put that guy in your movie?" the driver asked.

"Thought I'd give it one more try," Connor said. "I'd like to talk to him."

"You know, sometimes," the bus driver told him, "folks on this bus are just riding for a one-time only thing. They're not regulars or anything. They get on, and ride a few stops, and get off, and I never see 'em again. That's probably what this is." Connor must have looked discouraged, because the driver said, "So maybe you don't find him. Maybe your movie is about looking instead of finding."

Yeah, Connor thought. Maybe so.

He got out at the next stop. Standing on the sidewalk, looking back through the glass doors, he waved at the driver. "Hey," he said, "my girlfriend told me something about blue windows in city buses, like the color at night is this really cool blue. But that's not how this bus is. Am I just looking at the wrong kind of bus?"

The driver smiled, took his foot from the brake, then flicked a switch beneath the steering wheel. The bus windows blazed up blue, a deep glowing turquoise, a blue like swimming pool water at night, lit from below. Connor stood only a moment in wonder. Then he started filming.

So. How are you holding up? Are you getting tired of all this?

Tired of all what?

The questions, the photos and videos, sitting for paintings, being someone's project?

You know me. Anything for Art.

Good.

To be honest it does feel a little weird to be objectified like this but on another level it's kind of interesting. Plus I'm enjoying seeing what you come up with.

Yeah. Actually I'm feeling a little bit stuck the last week or so. Running out of ideas, maybe.

I have that sleep study tomorrow night. Maybe you could use that. Could be some interesting images.

Remind me what it's for?

Some kind of dream research clinical study. I don't know what it's all about. I never do. I just show up and do what they tell me. Kind of like The Connor Project.

Oh I see.

No, seriously, this one is easy. It's at the Sleep Center and as far as I understand it all I have to do is get wired into an EKG or something and then go to sleep. The ad said they were looking for people who have vivid dreams. I get seventy-five bucks just for spending the night.

Well. If you're sure you won't mind, maybe I'll tag along. I'm foreseeing two more pieces, maybe three.

And then The Connor Project is finished?

Probably.

How will you know?

I'll just know.

And then you'll just stop?

Yes. And then I'll just stop painting new pieces, just cut it off. Because if I don't, I'll be stuck on Connor forever and I'll never move on to anything new.

Move on to anything new.

Um–hmm.

I'm not so crazy about the sound of that, Boo.

Well. Yes. I understand that. I want to talk to you about something, actually.

Oh.

Connor. Have you ever thought about living somewhere else?

Sometimes. Yeah.

But you never have. You've lived here all your life.

Yes. This is home. I grew up here. My family is here. I'm comfortable here.

Too comfortable. That's sort of my point. You're stagnating here, Connor. And I am too. It's not good for our art.

What are you trying to tell me?… Boo?

I have to sell the house, Connor.

This house? Why?

It's half his, and it doesn't make sense for him to keep paying half the mortgage every month when he's not even living here. And I can't afford to buy it from him. So I've got to put it on the market.

When?

He wants to list it this month.… Even if it sells right away I'd still have a 30-day grace period before I had to move out.

This is all so sudden.

It had to happen sooner or later.

Well. I'm a little taken aback, but…. Look. I mean, I sort of had it in the back of my mind anyway that we might want to move in together. You know? I know we haven't really talked about it, but…. And I like this house. Maybe we could sit down and crunch some numbers? I don't know what my half of the payment would be, but—

I'd love to live with you. I really would. I think we're great together. But it's like I said: we're stagnating here. We have got to get out of this town. I want to live somewhere where there's a bigger art scene, more galleries, more studios, a bigger arts community.

You sound pretty determined.

I know. I'm sorry.

You're leaving, Boo? You're leaving?

Would you want to go with me?

I don't want to leave. I want you to stay here with me.

That's what I thought you'd say.

What's wrong with that? Is there something wrong with that?

No. It's very sweet, and I'm very tempted. It would be a lovely thing, living with you.

I think so too. We're good for each other.

I've never doubted that, babe.

So you'll think about it?… Boo?

Okay.

Yes?

Okay, Connor. I'll think about it. Yes.

Connor, Dreaming

In the last few moments of the clinical trial sleep study Connor was dreaming, a somehow familiar chase-and-flee narrative: a broken bicycle, rutted streets and burnt-out buildings, bad guys throwing rocks, and clinging with her warm arms around him was a woman he'd met only hours before. With dream-certainty he knew it was Renee, his nurse-technician, even though she looked and sounded exactly like Sheridan Boudreaux. "Pedal faster," Renee whispered to him, "just a little farther, we're getting there." And Connor, fearful and aroused, pedaled. They flew down a long hill and through a red light, tires screeching, car horns honking. They leaned into curves. Renee laid her cheek on the back of his neck and eased her hand under his shirt. Connor strained to hear what she said.

What she said was, "Mr. Connor? Good morning. Time to wake up."

As the dream dissipated Connor realized her voice was coming not from the woman behind him on the bicycle but from the intercom of his clinic bedroom, and with that realization he rolled over and squinted at the speaker and said, thickly, "Good morning."

"I'll be right in to unhook you," Renee's voice said. "Just sit tight."

She was there a moment later carrying a styrofoam cup of coffee, smiling, wearing light blue scrubs and jogging shoes, and she patted Connor on the shoulder. "Sleep well?"

"About as well as could be expected, all wired up like this," Connor told her.

"We'll have you disconnected in no time," she said. She pulled up a chair and began gently detaching electrodes from his head. "Tell me if I hurt you, okay?"

"You won't," Connor said. He gazed directly into her pale eyes; she was looking slightly to the side, removing a sensor from his right temple. She smelled pleasantly of coffee and soap, and her hands on him were quick and sure. Connor blinked, thinking about the way she'd wrapped herself around him on the back of the bike.

"I was having such a vivid dream a few minutes ago," he said.

"I noticed." She grinned. "You were in hyper-REM."

"You could see that?"

"Oh, sure. Needles off the charts. Must have been a good one! I hated to wake you up."

Embarrassed, he flashed on an image of Renee at her video monitor, watching the two of them on the bicycle, and he was glad she'd awakened him before things had gotten out of hand. Then he wondered irrationally if she had implanted and controlled the dream herself—sending some kind of electrical code through the wires, uploading images and episodes directly into his cortex. He felt suddenly shy. To change the subject he said, "These things come off easier than I expected."

"You have good skin," she said.

"*You* have good skin," Connor said. "It's beautiful. You must hear that all the time."

Renee actually blushed. "Oh, that's silly. I do not."

"I'm serious," Connor said. He was telling the truth. Renee's looks were otherwise unremarkable, but her skin was gorgeous. "You have this glow about you."

"Well," she said. "If you say so. Maybe it's the baby."

With sudden slow dawning—what an idiot, he thought, to have missed it!—Connor saw that under her baggy blue top she was indeed pregnant.

"They say you get this healthy glow in the first trimester," she explained.

"Congratulations," Connor said.

Pregnant. That was why. Here we go again, he thought.

Connor and Boo had come in an hour late the night before, and while wiring him up Renee had grumbled teasingly about problem patients who kept her from getting her work done on time. She made no objection to Boo and her digital camera, even when Boo stopped the procedure every few minutes to take her photographs or ask her questions ("What sort of adhesive are you using on the electrodes?" "We just call it glue."). "It's kind of a documentary," Connor explained to Renee, but Boo snorted and said it wasn't any kind of a documentary, it was just photographs of Connor.

"Well, people do take all kinds of pictures," Renee told them. "Surgical scars, tumors, all kinds of things. For their scrapbooks or something, I guess."

"I think a sleep study is an interesting metaphor," Boo said. "Or it could be, depending on how it's presented. Are you sleepy, Connor?"

"Getting there."

In a chair a few feet down from them a fat man in late middle age was having electrodes attached to his Santa Claus beard. His technician was a young man with an exasperated lisp. Connor saw the tableaux as classic barber shop: a line of chairs, barbers making small talk over their clients. The fat man began to say something, then went into a protracted coughing fit. His technician sighed. "This god-blesséd chin sensor thing isn't sticking, Renee," he announced.

"Sometimes beards can be tricky. We might have to shave him."

"The hell you say," the fat man gasped. Boo asked him if she could take his photograph. He was wearing gray gym shorts and a thin and faded undershirt that could not cover his huge hairy belly, and Connor knew Boo found him grotesque and therefore eminently worth shooting. "Ain't every day a man gets his pitcher took by a purdy lady," the man said, and nodded at her: "Go 'head on."

Boo took a few shots of the technician pressing the sensor to the man's chin. Then she turned back to Connor, snapping several extreme closeups. By that time he was wired like a Christmas tree: a dozen electrodes on his head, two on his chest and two on his legs. The wire from each fed into a harness plug, which Connor held for Renee as she made the last connections.

"Your wife is interesting," Renee said, after Boo had left. She was kneeling to re-attach a wayward electrode to Connor's calf. She pressed with both thumbs.

"She's my girlfriend."

"Oh. Well, are y'all going to get married?"

"I don't know. Maybe. We've both been married before, though, and at least for the moment we're feeling kind of anti-marriage."

"Hmpf." She pursed her lips and Connor wondered if he'd offended her. She was not wearing a ring, but he'd noticed little jewelry on any of the technicians; maybe they weren't allowed to wear it. Renee took the harness from him and carefully began straightening some kinked wires, tugging and untangling. "What will she do with them?" she asked.

"The photos? She'll take them back to her studio and blow them up and print them out. Then she'll throw random blobs of paint at them or maybe cut them into lots of pieces, like big puzzles, and glue them back at awkward angles."

"I read about this artist who painted with urine," Renee said. "Also there was a lady on TV a few years ago who was teaching horses to paint with their noses. They would dip their noses into the paint and then rub up against the canvas."

Connor decided not to debate the aesthetic merits

of horse art. He watched Renee plug in the harness and adjust a dial.

"Almost done," she said. "Now we just have to get a baseline reading, and then we can put you to bed."

Wondering whether she was flirting, he tried to catch her eye. But she was bending over a clipboard, annotating a checklist, and Connor realized that in some ways, in his teeshirt and pajama pants and with his mussed-up hair, he must resemble the man in the next chair, that he was now just another patient in for a sleep study. He'd gone to bed feeling blue, a little world-weary, and it seemed to him that he'd hardly shut his eyes before she was calling his name.

"I feel like I tossed and turned all night," Connor said now.

"You pretty much did," Renee said, reaching into his pajama leg to detach the calf electrodes. She slid the tangle of wires into her smock pocket; no ring, he noticed again. "All done."

"So how did I do?"

"Great. Good baseline and very usable readings. We got what we needed."

"Thanks, Renee," Connor said, "thanks for taking care of me."

"No problem," she told him. At the door she turned and wiggled her fingers at him, like waving to a little kid. "Just stop by the front desk on your way out, and take care now, you hear?"

The mailbox in front of Boo's house read SHERIDAN BOU-DREAUX and as he swung into the driveway, too fast, Connor nearly sideswiped it. He killed the engine and set the parking brake, then sat for a moment looking out the window. The barren tulip tree in Boo's front yard was trussed in toilet paper and it stood white and tortured against the grayish sky like some pathetic maypole. "Meanwhile, back at the ranch," Connor said, and got out.

In her studio Boo was bending over a series of big printouts of Connor's face. He could tell she'd been working through the night. She wore a paint-spattered white undershirt and cowboy boots and a plaid pair of flannel boxers she'd swiped from Connor's laundry basket, and her long thick hair was held back off her face with a big brown clip and there was paint under her nails and a smudge of ochre on her cheek. It cheered Connor to see her, she was so quirky and odd and funny. He wanted to throw his arms around her. Instead, he said, "You know your yard got rolled again?"

"Them s'rority sluts acrost the street," Boo said in mock despair. "Why them girls hates me, I got no idee. Reckon I best set the law on 'em."

"Telefoam the sherf," Connor said, playing along.

"Um hmm." Boo set down her brush. "So how did it go?"

"Good," he said. "And they paid me on the way out."

"Yay." She smiled, scrunching up her eyes at him. "Let me just finish up a few little bits here and there and then we can celebrate."

Connor settled back to watch. It always amazed him how fast Boo was, how sure her moves were. The piece she was working on, he saw, was a triptych: a long rectangle of brown paper featuring three inset printouts, life-sized, of Connor's wired-up head. One shot was a profile; one was portrait; and the last showed Connor and Renee face to face. In all the shots the yellow, green, and orange wires sprouted from his head Medusa-like. He noticed a hazy soft-focus quality to the images and asked about it. "First I did a Gaussian blur in Photoshop," Boo said, without looking up. "Then I printed them out. Then while the ink was drying I threw them in the bathtub and ran water over them." It looked to Connor as if she had also crumpled each portrait, then re-flattened it, then pasted it down to the brown paper. She was now scribbling over top of each image with a piece of untinted wax crayon, bold and violent scrawls and X's. Repeatedly she slashed at Renee's face, leaving no visible marks. Finally she stood back and looked for a moment, then picked up a cup of thin green acrylic and poured it carefully over the images; the paint bled away from the wax so that the image underneath showed through a green gouache. Boo blotted with paper towels.

"Let's go lie down," she said, "while that dries."

In bed Connor couldn't seem to connect. He felt diffused, scattered. His attention seemed elsewhere. Above him Boo kissed his closed eyes, his nose, his mouth; then she was laughing, running her hands through his hair and laughing. "You need a shampoo, baby," she said; she'd found the dried clumps of electrode adhesive stuck on his scalp. Connor laughed with her, rolled her over, nuzzled her neck, rested his head on her breasts. The room was bright with mid-morning sunlight. After a few moments he found his focus and they began again, and this time Connor put his heart into it. He and Boo were usually like old friends, comfortable and easy as a faded pair of jeans, but sometimes he realized that he also loved her fiercely, intensely, almost overwhelmingly; she was everything to him in a way that she, with her art career and her slightly ironic distance, could only partly reciprocate. Those feelings came to him now and he renewed his efforts with a kind of abandon and despair. He lost himself in her. He stopped thinking, he went out of his space for a while. And he took her with him.

"Love, love, love," Boo murmured in his ear some time later. Connor, lying very still, felt her breath on his neck and her breasts on his back; she was curled around him, and she lazily ran her bare foot over his foot, the way you'd pet a cat with your foot, he thought. He didn't want to move. He was drained, drowsy. Boo asked if he wanted to take a nap.

"Maybe."

"I bet you didn't sleep a wink all wired up like that."

"It wasn't the wires," Connor said. "It was the dreams. I had all these weird dreams, Boo."

"Tell me."

Connor thought. He started slowly, feeling his way.

"I dreamed I was riding this bicycle…. This old, weird bike made out of bits and pieces of other bikes…. And you were riding with me." Like now, he thought. "You were behind me, just like now, holding on to me, exactly like this."

"Mmm," Boo said.

"There were all these people after us. Throwing rocks, yelling. We were trying to get away." Connor considered. "And you were pregnant, Boo. I could feel your tummy."

"Pregnant!" Boo said. "How could you tell? How do you know I wasn't just fat?"

"I could tell. You know how you know things in dreams."

"Yes. But pregnant…. Well, I'm not, so you don't have to worry about it."

"But I wasn't worried about it, Boo. Neither of us was. We were happy about it, that's the weird thing. It was like the most natural thing in the world."

"Is there more?"

"We went to the hospital," Connor said. "That's where we had been heading on the bike. We went in, and you had the baby. It just popped out like a little doll or something. And we wrapped it up and took it home."

Boo seemed to sigh.

"We were really happy," Connor murmured.

"You're scaring me," she said.

"Maybe we should talk about that," Connor said.

"There's no reason to talk about it. We've talked

about it plenty, and kids are not in the cards for us. You know that."

"Okay." Connor closed his eyes. "I know that. Yeah."

"Turn over here, David," she said. "Look at me, okay?"

He did. She searched his eyes for some time. Then she took him in hand and kissed him and they began again.

When they were finished, Connor was wiped out and said so. He felt himself drifting, falling deeper into her feather pillows, the heavy air slowing and stalling around him. He heard Boo breathing and he synched his breath with hers. His jaw went slack. As he faded into sleep the last image that came to his mind's eye was the tulip tree covered in toilet paper. Around it he saw a dozen near-naked young women—were they sorority girls?—dancing in some kind of fertility rite. They touched themselves; they tossed their hair and thrust their hips. Connor, dreaming, sat and watched; he marveled. The women waved and blew kisses at him and then one by one began changing into babies—fat, happy babies. The babies cooed and crawled and beckoned to him, and Connor felt again his unaccountable sorrow. But there was consolation: it was just a dream, just random neurons firing, and it didn't mean anything at all, and the reason he knew that was because Boo stood beside him, holding his hand, and told him so.

five

Epilogue: The Connor Project

Connor in Utero
Acrylic on canvas, 2006

The vivid reds and blacks and the jagged white slash in the left foreground suggest the darkness of the womb occasionally punctuated by flashes of bright light (obstetrician's lamp? sunbathing?). The dark circular motifs call to mind bubbles, swooshing sounds, gurgles, a time when life was liquid.

The inspiration for this painting comes from a remark (perhaps in jest?) that David Connor made not long after meeting the artist. Although he was born over 40 years ago (1964), Connor claims to retain vivid prenatal memories: "I was happy in there, damn it. My whole life has been a quest to get back there."

Sibling Rivalry
Mixed media: photograph, calligraphy pen,
and acrylic on canvas, 2006

Connor's sister Terri, a successful regional musician in the lesbian rock genre, was born two years after Connor, "just in time," she says, "to save him from growing up a spoiled brat." In this piece, the family photograph is inset in the right foreground: a three-year-old Connor holding his year-old sister, a sour look on his face. The calligraphy section reflects the artist's strong interest in graphic design; in seven languages (Arabic, Hindi, English, Russian, Japanese, and Finnish) it repeats the phrase "just in time, a spoiled brat." The painted section shows the roles reversed: Connor as infant and Terri as toddler. There are faint suggestions here of Madonna and Child, Connor as Christ-figure.

Allison, Amanda, Ashley, Belinda, Candi, Caryl, Christine, Davin, Ellen....
Mixed media: digitally manipulated photographs, aluminum track, 2006
VIEWER PARTICIPATION INVITED

Recalling pocket puzzles of childhood—lettered tiles mounted in a plastic frame, the tiles sliding vertically or horizontally to simultaneously fill an empty space and empty a filled space—this 7 x 7 foot grid of photographs of 49 former girlfriends and lovers is arranged so that they can be read alphabetically (left to right), chronologically (red numbers stenciled into each frame), or by more idiosyncratic criteria, such eye or hair color (the ratio of blondes to redheads, for example, encourages speculation). Mixed in with the 6" square photos are some of Connor's blurred shots of mannequin heads, an element that adds ambiguity: is it a comment on his misogyny? a statement on his presumed love of the female form? a random design element? As viewers rearrange Allison, Amanda, Ashley, *et al,* the puzzle pieces begin to reflect the unreliable nature of memory and the eventual triumph of romantic chaos. Photos courtesy of David Connor.

"Because I Wanted A Baby, And He Didn't"
Digitally manipulated photo collage and acrylic paint on canvas, 2006

Connor was married once, for two years, four months, and eight days, after which time he and his wife Hope filed for an uncontested divorce. During her *Connor Project* research, the artist taped dozens of hours of interviews with friends, family, and exes. In this triptych of Hope Connor (*née* Powell) we see three closely-spaced instants captured on film, and we note the shape of her mouth as she pronounces the plosive *B* in *Because*, the soft *W* in *wanted*, and the close-teethed hiss of the *H* in *he*. Hope's explanation of why the marriage fell apart is undercut by the bottom third of the canvas, where photos of Terri, Connor's mother, and Connor's father are mounted under three calligraphed sentences actually recorded by the artist: "That's a load of horseshit," "That girl was too snooty for David," and "I only met her once."

So Why Did They Kill Socrates?
Encaustic and video on canvas, 2007

The background is gray and black acrylic paint mixed with wax: textured encaustic. On the right is a white rectangle acting as a screen for a black-and-white video emitted from a ceiling-mount projector. The video is a loop of an old man wearing a white shirt and a dark tie; standing before a chalkboard, he says over and over, "So why did they kill Socrates?" On the word "why," he jabs at the viewer with what appears to be a piece of chalk. On the word "Socrates" he raises his left eyebrow. A different male voice is mixed under the old man's; also a loop, it says, almost inaudibly, "I always wanted to be my father." Video courtesy of David Connor.

Mother and Son
Acrylic paint and snapshots on canvas, 2007

An adult Connor stands holding hands with his mother. He wears jeans and an untucked brown shirt and he looks straight ahead. His mother also wears jeans and a brown tanktop; she is gazing at her son. The stylized figures are soft-edged, almost blurred, and the colors are muted. Across the bottom of the painting is a series of six snapshots of Connor and his mother at various ages, arranged chronologically from left to right: Connor being breastfed; Connor's mother bending and blowing at birthday candles with a five-year-old Connor; Connor and mom at his wedding, etc. Photos courtesy of Adele Collington Connor.

Connor (Nude No. 1)
Acrylic paint on canvas, 2007

The figure stands casually beside a window filled with blue bottles; azure sunlight coming through the bottles falls on his hip, his chest, and one side of his face. His eyes are closed, as a figure in rapture, and his arms are stretched wide, one slightly raised, one slightly lowered, in a pose suggestive, perhaps, of crucifixion. His belly is soft and hints at a certain laxness. His chest hair is starting to gray, as is his pubic hair. His phallus, ambiguous, uncertain, seems half-erect.

"There's Not A Day That I Don't Think About It"
Acrylic paint on canvas, 2006

Another "dark" painting, the background is black and gray and the lettering is white. At the top left corner in block letters are the words "baby names." In a column down the left side in bright white paint are the words "Aaron," "Abigail," "Adam," "Alisha," "Amy," etc., one name per row. Near the middle of the painting, between "Lorian" and "Mark," the white letters begin to fade and the names blend into the black. The right hand columns feature names becoming darker and darker—"Tammy, Thomas, Ursula," until the lower right corner of the canvas is nothing but darkness.

Connor, Dreaming
*Digitally-manipulated photo collage, acrylic paint,
colored pencil, and encaustic, 2007*

Connor's face, twice life size, is repeated thrice, establishing a rhythmical pattern to the design. A dozen electrodes and their attendant wires sprout from his head, each a different color. Over the photos a series of gestural shapes have been scrawled in pencil, paint, and wax, and the piece has been subjected to fire, water, earth, and air (respectively, the scorched left side burnt by butane lighter; the middle and part of the right photograph spilled with iced tea; the upper right corner smeared with mud; and the entire piece airbrushed with clear acrylic lacquer). The EKG scroll across the bottom is a four-foot section of Connor's actual readout from his sleep study. The expressions on the three faces of Connor vary from boredom, alertness, and gently smiling interest.

Connor (Nude No. 2)
Acrylic paint on canvas, 2007

Though there is less than a year between the completion of this painting and the "Nude No. 1," it is clear that the figure here has aged. His expression is resigned, perhaps fatalistic. And yet it is not an unhappy image; he seems calm and strong. A hint of a crinkle plays around the corners of his eyes. He sits with his back to the window, this time with his hands modestly arranged over his lap, mostly hiding his flaccid phallus. The blue bottles glint. And to the side, faintly reflected in a dressing mirror: a shimmering light-drenched bare-breasted woman, smiling.

About The Artist

Sheridan Boudreaux was born in Shreveport, Louisiana, and attended Pratt (BFA) and The Cooper School for Art (MFA Painting). She has exhibited her work in one-woman shows in New York, Los Angeles, and many other cities. She is the recipient of many grants and awards, including the 1999-2000 International Woman Millennium Award, an *ART NEWS* citation for mixed media composition, and a Sara Elizabeth Collins Grant from the American Academy of the Arts. She has recently moved to Atlanta, Georgia, with her collection of blue Depression glass, two Siamese fighting fish named Jackson and Lee, and David Connor.

Acknowledgements

I'm grateful to many folks for encouragement, inspiration, and love during the writing of this book: Erica Plouffe Lazure, who knows all the good stories; Peter Makuck, Terry Davis, and Erwin Hester, who set me on this path; Alex Albright, Mary Carroll-Hackett, David Dickson, Mark Johnson, Amy Willoughby-Burle, and the late Bill Hallberg, fellow travelers; Peter Dawyot of the Publicus Community and Emily Forsberg of MLE Creative, for *The Connor Project* cover; Robert Cumming and Beto Cumming of Iris Press, for their support of my work both past and present; and Wildacres Retreat, The Virginia Center for the Creative Arts, and The Hambidge Center, for residencies during which I wrote and revised this book.

And many thanks to you.

Some of these pieces were previously published in the following journals:

> "Before Breakfast" in *The MacGuffin*.
> "Connor's Story" in *New Virginia Review*; reprinted as "Loflin's Story" in *Frank: An International Journal of the Arts* (France).
> "Background" in *Racing Home: New Stories by Award-Winning North Carolina Writers*.
> "Castro, Mi Amor" and "River of Time" in *The Raleigh News & Observer*'s "Sunday Journal."
> "Meta-mannequin" and "University Billiards" in *The Dos Passos Review*.
> "Up" in *NEO: Revista* (Portugal).
> "Dark-Haired Girl in a Red Pickup Truck" in *Gander Press Review*.
> "Two Years and Seventeen Months" in *PerContra*.

CPSIA information can be obtained
at www.ICGtesting.com
Printed in the USA
LVHW041321270322
714518LV00007B/1268